THE DANCE
OF SOULS

Romina Caruana

ISBN:978-0-9909909-0-1

Library of Congress Control Number

Published by Mimi Tales Productions

www.rominacaruana.com

Printed in the United States of America

ENDORSEMENTS

"Books are my bedtime friends, no matter the genre or theme. I always read a few pages of a good book before turning off the light. But in the case of *The Dance of Souls*, the ten minutes I usually spend reading have stretched to all night; I could not stop reading before the last page. It's not only a well-written and overwhelming book, but also valuable for Romina's exploration of the subject of autism, a disorder that has always struck me as a mysterious evil, which is scary and very human at the same time. The book of Caruana works in two directions: while you are reading it, it reads you, too."

~ **Franco Nero**, *Actor*

"I appreciated the lightness and the lack of victimism. *The Dance of Souls,* in a memorable, haunting and suggestive Sicily, is a very feminine and sensual book that captures your attention even after reading it."

~ **Vincenzo Amato,** *Actor, Sculptor*

"I read your book with tears in my eyes…It caused a storm inside of me and brought to the surface a lot of emotions that I daily try to keep under control. You have no idea how much I saw of myself in both Eleonora and Letizia. It seemed as if I was reading about my life…Thank you for sharing your story. I needed to hear the words of the wise indian. Maybe one day I'll be able to purify myself as well…"

~ **Cristina I.,** *mother of an autistic child.*

"Romina has penned an inspiring story about autism and her brother's journey navigating through this mysterious disease. As she writes in *The Dance of Souls*, there are numerous facets to autism including behavioral, medical and emotional, and she deals with all of them in way that will encourage and inspire parents and other family members of autistic children."

~ **David Dunham,** *Publisher*

"This deeply moving and poetic story is one of survival, redemption, self-discovery and acceptance. A breathless illustration of our human bonds and how they mold our very essence. From autism to transcendence, these souls embody the dance."

~ **Wendi Morrison,** *Musician, Environmental Advocate*

"Knowing Romina as a person it was only half of the story: as an actress she revealed herself as a multifaceted rare gem."

~ **Enrico Mastracchi Manes**, *Producer*

"I met Romina at a film festival in Georgia. Her eyes had that sparkle that you seldom see; when you do, however, you know that person has a love of life that will guarantee success in whatever they choose to do. I read Romina's book, *The Dance of Souls* ten months later and realized that the sparkle in the eyes emanated from her loving heart and her beautiful soul".

~ **Bob Saporiti,** *Senior Vice President International Marketing / General Manager Warner Bros. Records*

"*The Dance of Souls* is at once a treasure trove of luminescent poetry, a fascinating education about the mystery of autism, and a practical psychological 'How to' manual for turning the raw material of meaningless suffering in this life, into the priceless gold of purpose filled transcendence. In this wonderful book Romina Caruana reignites our heart's latent knowledge concerning the alchemy of love."

~ **Keith Merritt,** *Screenwriter*

"Romina tells her story with a very sensitive touch. The same sensitive touch I have experienced on the set by knowing her as an actress."

~ **Carlo Siliotto,** *Composer, Golden Globe nomination*

"In this evocative, tender, and masterfully written book, Ms. Caruana has managed to give a very human voice to autism while giving us a personal narrative that serves to move and inspire and, most importantly, illuminate a disease that has for too long lived in the shadows. It is a brave work. Told with humor and heart, *The Dance of Souls* truly shows how great pain 'can be transformed into light and joy for life.' Autism is not a curse. And we can all learn, while being entertained, from this beautiful book."

~ **Spencer Garrett,** *Actor*

"After working with the talented Romina Caruana for two years, I can say that she brings expansion to the roles she plays, her choices as an actress are always on target and interesting."

~ **Nikkolas Rey,** *Theatrical Agent*

INTRODUCTION

For years I investigated autism, analyzing every article that discussed the subject in the hope of understanding what was hidden behind the complex, compromised, and yet deeply joyful personality of my autistic brother.

What could I do to help him?

I spent years trying to grasp the sense of it, embarking on spiritual journeys and various types of therapy until I eventually understood that it was not my brother who did not exist, but rather myself. During this voyage of self-discovery and awareness, where the scientific and spiritual worlds intersect, I have encountered extraordinary people worthy of endless respect. A single phrase has touched my heart and my life more than anything else, comforting me and contributing to my survival: "Autistic children are angels fallen from the sky who don't want to come down to earth."

With this book, I want to show how great pain can be transformed into light and joy for life. Autism is not a curse. If we shift our perspective and find a higher point of view, we may yet realize that these angels have come to teach us something. Today I am certain that my brother has been my greatest teacher and hero, and I am proud that he chose me to be his sister. I would like to express my gratitude to my family, because all the suffering endured has taught me so much.

Romina Caruana

For Fabrizio.
For Roberta.
For Ivan.
For Mimì.

To all the angels fallen from the sky.

"All happy families are alike; every unhappy family is unhappy in its own way."

~ Leo Tolstoy, Anna Karenina

"The time has come for people to direct their spiritual awareness also downward into matter, into everything they do: work, education, family life, friendship, their communications with strangers, the way they build their home. To all the most mundane, practical aspects of daily human life. People need now to become God-centered from within, and from that center to see God everywhere, in everything."

~ **Swami Kriyananda** (J. Donald Walters)
Cities of Light

Tu sei il mio cielo, figlio, ed io
il tuo mare.
Quando sorride nell'azzurro il sole,
il mar se ne fa tutto illuminare;
e quando tra le nubi il ciel si duole
con lacrime di pioggia, il mare
affranto
tutto raccoglie su di sé quel pianto

Alba Scialla

Translation

You are my heaven, my son, and I your sea.

When the sun smiles in the blue,

the sea lets everything become sparkling;

and when among clouds, the sky grieves with tears of rain,

the heartbroken sea collects all those tears on himself.

~ **Alba Scialla**

TABLE OF CONTENTS

PREFACE

A journey. A journey of knowledge toward awareness; a journey of discovery through sharing a brother's destiny, a destiny that affects every individual member in the family: autism.

Romina Caruana's novel is set in a separate, often isolated world that loudly demands love and attention, answers and solutions, for an illness still considered mysterious and unknowable today. It is a heartfelt and engaging narrative that relates the difficulties experienced by all families touched by autism. The story is presented from an original and unusual viewpoint—that of a sister whose personal history of feelings, dreams, and projects has also been affected by the illness. The main character, Eleonora, researches, challenges, and battles with her brother's disorder—an unknown, unnamed, and fear-evoking illness—against the backdrop of the avoidant and patriarchal society of Sicily, which avoids, rebuffs, and condemns it.

It is surprising to find the scientific research that the

author presents on autism in such a breathtaking narrative—one that demands to be read, understood, and shared. Interwoven into the narrative are detailed descriptions of recent research on autism, as well as alternative therapies offered by biomedical treatment and the "Defeat Autism Now!" (DAN!) method. The research that the author discusses within the story is the product of her profound personal knowledge and in-depth scientific research, fed by her desire to understand the problem, and a focus on and a fusion with the essence of the soul of her autistic brother. The focus is always on the person before the illness and the spirit before the body, and she makes this perspective available to all of us.

This voyage of knowledge is also a journey of self-awareness for Eleonora; through her experience with the disorder, she overcomes her limits and embarks on a spiritual journey of growth that leads her to the final answer—*The Dance of Souls* that finds completion through love and the gift of oneself.

Nicola Antonucci, Psychiatrist, DAN!

Curriculum Vitae

Dr. Nicola Antonucci is a preeminent Italian luminary on the subject of treating autism. He graduated in medicine from the University of Bari, where he also completed his specialization in Psychiatry. During that time, he worked at the

Psychiatric Neurosciences Group of the Psychiatric Institute at Bari Polyclinic, researching functional and spectroscopic MRI studies on cognitive deficits in schizophrenia patients while also contributing to international publications. Since October 2006, when his daughter was diagnosed with autism spectrum disorder (ASD), he started to work with biomedical treatment of ASDs using the knowledge and methods of the Autism Research Institute in San Diego, California. He trained for several months at the The Rimland Centre in Lynchburg, Virginia under the mentoring of Dr Elizabeth Mumper. He still attends annual scientific meetings and training sessions of the Autism Research Institute.

He is now director of the Biomedical Centre for Autism Research and Treatment in Bari, Italy, and works exclusively with children affected by ASDs in several Italian towns, as well as a number of countries. In 2010, in collaboration with Dr. Dario Siniscalco of the Second University of Naples, he founded a research group to study molecular and cellular changes in ASDs. This group is conducting research trials and has already published works in international peer-reviewed journals.

SIROCCO

That winter afternoon, the purple-tinted clouds coming off the Mediterranean Sea suddenly darkened over the brightly colored garden of the villa. The lemon and orange trees quickly lost their green highlights, and were instead daubed in the grey and purple hues brought by the clouds. The tornado, which had blown up in the open sea, approached unexpectedly, bringing rain and lightning. The sirocco wind, as deafening and menacing as the howls of wolves in the night, was already bending the tall pines and palm trees with the blows of its whip, and now began to unhinge the shutters flanking the large drawing room. To the frightened eyes of eight-year-old Eleonora, the blowing shutters were reminiscent of open mouths ready to devour prey. Splinters were flying everywhere, glass shattering to fragments on the floor. Tossed about in the fierce wind, Grandmother Alba's pale, embroidered, antique curtains ripped and tore. The porthole was swinging, the silk threads of the ceiling light were all tangled up, and the grand piano was covered in desert sand and mud.

Letizia, Eleonora's mother, had hair white with dust and a wounded heart. It was all over in the arc of several minutes. Eleonora did not understand her mother's cries of "Lord! Help me!" as she tried to hold back the shutters, too heavy for her fragile figure. Her Grandmother Maddalena covered Eleonora with a shawl to protect her from the detritus and also from the sight of that terrible damage. "It's the end of the world!" whispered Maddalena in despair. "I'm dying!"

And it did feel like the end of the world. Was the tornado an omen? What was the meaning of a house that rebelled against its own insides? "Go and telephone Papa right away" shouted Letizia. Maddalena and Eleonora ran into the kitchen. "Mamma says that you have to come home straightaway," said the little girl, "there's a tornado blowing here and everything is breaking! Call the police!" "Don't worry, my darling, your mother always exaggerates! I'm on my way!" answered Luigi.

By the time the wailing sirens of the fire brigade reached them, Letizia, Eleonora, and Maddalena were exhausted, observing in silence the aftermath of such violent destruction. "The ship is about to sink; you must leave the villa!" the fire chief called through his loudhailer from the garden. Letizia replied that she would not leave her house for anything in the world. Eleonora would have happily abandoned the house. She felt there was something sinister in the house, something that was refusing them.

Luigi had built Villa Letizia to show off his hard-won wealth, to make an impression on people, and it was opulent and oversized. There may have been no hot water or heating in the winter, but Luigi didn't care about that. It was known in the town as "the house of Doctor Luigi Calabrò." They didn't have the staff required for its upkeep, so Letizia was kept busy cleaning from morning to night. Cinderella by day, she transformed in the evenings when she changed for parties or to go to the theatre, becoming the extremely elegant and charming Lady Letizia. She knew how to please Luigi, who always wanted her to be beautiful in public.

On the heels of the blazing sirens, Luigi finally arrived. He managed to clear a pathway through the fallen trees in the garden to the house. "No drama here, Chief. You can go. Tomorrow we will clean all this up and that will be the end of it." He turned to his family and said, "Off to bed now, quickly. Tomorrow I have to get up early."

"Can I sleep in your bed?" asked Eleonora.

"Of course" said her father, "but only for tonight."

THE TURKISH STEPS
The Scala dei Turchi

The next day, none of them mentioned the event; it was to be forgotten, exiled through silence. While to the curious, the calamity was described in detail, within the family no mention was permitted; no occasion for sharing perspectives was allowed. Eleonora would have liked to cry, but she had decided that it would be best not to do it in front of her parents. She had once cried in the kitchen and her father Luigi had remonstrated, "Stop playing the victim; I know you're only crying to get some attention." The little girl had stopped immediately, and from that day on she realized it was best to "play the victim" elsewhere. So she took herself off to the *Scala dei Turchi*, the Turkish Steps, close to her house. It was one of the most delightful places her eyes had ever seen—a rock formation of blindingly white limestone that stood overlooking the sea in a series of stratified platforms, one above the other, which appeared to bear witness to centuries long gone.

Eleonora walked across the wild beach, torched by the sun, which lead to the bottom of the *marl*[1] rock. The limestone looked like a mountain of blinding white snow diving directly into the sea, as if nature had mistakenly placed it at the wrong latitude. *How can the snow not melt in this Sicilian heat?* she wondered. She climbed to the top and began to scream with all her strength at the sea, the very same sea that had allowed the tornado to invade her home. The burning sun painted the evening sky with violet streaks. She screamed as loudly as she could, spinning round and round in a dizzying whirl and fell exhausted onto the pure white ground.

---

[1] The marl is a sedimentary rock, terrigenous type, composed of a clay fraction. A fraction of the carbonate is generally supplied by calcium carbonate (calcite), or bicarbonate of calcium and magnesium (dolomite). This type of rock comes from muddy sediment, mainly of marine origin, set down in conditions of low energy of the medium. The clay component is deposited by slow settling of clay particles.

AZURE BEACH
Lido Azzurro

Several years earlier, Luigi, Letizia, and Eleonora had lived in a little villa on the beach in *Lido Azzurro*. It was known as Villino Maddalena. Calogero, Luigi's father, had bought it a few years before his death and named it after his wife. It had the look of Greek-island houses and was as blindingly white as the Turkish Steps, with azure shutters that gave it a vivacious air. Eleonora was born there, in that house.

"A woman should know how to give birth," said Luigi to his wife, holding her hands tightly. But she was afraid. "You know how it's done, help me." Letizia stopped breathing, closed her eyes and, as she was preparing to die, then opened them with difficulty, contorted in pain. "Push; don't stop. You must find the strength." With a final cry, Eleonora was born at dawn, wrapped in a light summer breeze. In that isolated house by the sea, far from Agrigento, she was born in the way people used to be born, with a midwife, basins, wet cloths, and two grandmothers present—Maddalena and Alba, who hated each other. As soon as his daughter had come into the world, Luigi kissed his wife on her forehead and said, "I have to go to the hospital." He crossed the narrow corridor to the room that had been prepared to receive the new life. He stopped and gently rocked the crib. Sky blue. He stroked the little shoes, the bibs. Blue, all blue. He locked the door with a key, left the house, and finally, he breathed. Letizia, in her bed, also took a breath. Each to their own.

Letizia and Luigi had married a year before on her family's *masseria*.[2] On that festive day, the garden was lit up with dozens of flaming torches and immense candelabras. The orchestra played the hit songs from the late 1960s for the entertainment of the delighted guests, who danced all night. The couple left that night on their honeymoon, boarding a transatlantic liner at the port of Sciacca. Once aboard, Letizia's heart began to beat loudly; she had imagined the moment hundreds of times. Luigi took his wife's hand and lead her to their cabin. It would be the first time they made love. In a mix of embarrassment and excitement, they let their clothes fall to the floor. Kissing intensely, they lay down to feel every centimeter of the other's skin, getting to know each other through smell and touch. Their bodies began to pulse with sensations never felt before; the taste of their kisses

---

[2] Sicilian farmhouse at the center of an estate.

became a single fragrance. They loved each other for a long time, discovering the pleasure of belonging to each other. They remained entwined for two whole days, rocked by the sea, in love.

When they returned from the honeymoon two months later, Letizia was pregnant. They decided to hold a lunch at Villino Maddalena to announce the good news to Luigi's family. Luigi's siblings were there, Pino and Gina, with Pino's wife Sara and Gina's husband Nino. Maddalena was also there. They toasted happily, and Letizia began to tell Nino and Pino about the enchanting places they had visited in America, showing them the photographs taken on their trip. She told them how she had felt nauseous from the very first days of her pregnancy.

At the end of the meal, the women of the family, Maddalena, Gina and Sara, began to take the plates away and clean up, while Letizia remained seated, in conversation with her brothers in law. Luigi brusquely interrupted his wife, asking, "Can't you see the other women are taking away the plates? What are you waiting for? Go and help them."

"Yes, I'll do so in a moment," she replied. "I'll just finish the story and then I'll join them."

Luigi grabbed her arm with an angry movement, saying, "You'd find any excuse to avoid washing up. From today, you are to do what I say. You've been spoiled by your family."

No one had the courage to intervene in an argument between husband and wife; Letizia herself did not react in her own defense but obeyed without a word. She was in love with him and, for fear of not being loved back, she tried to please him in every way. Furthermore, she was carrying his child in her belly, and would never have wanted to put that at risk by becoming enraged.

The next day, the newlyweds were expected for lunch with Letizia's family. Aunt Carmelina would be there as well as Letizia's siblings, Ferdinando and Laura. However, Luigi decided that they were not going to attend. He made his wife tell them that she was feeling too unwell. This was the first in a long series of injustices that Letizia would bear in silence without ever telling anyone.

THE TEACHER
AND
THE GENTLEMAN
FARMER

Luigi had set his eyes on Letizia when she was still a child. Letizia's family came from an ancient feudatory estate, the richest and most noble of the entire Agrigento region. Luigi wasn't interested in the wealth, however; he simply wanted the most beautiful girl in the region. When Letizia went for her evening stroll in the square with Aunt Carmelina, Luigi would stare at her constantly. They exchanged languid, dreamy gazes. In secret, they professed their undying love. Letizia found him charming, confident, a star of the cinema screen. Luigi, though, was also possessive, forbidding her to go out once he had left town to return to Padua, where he studied for his specialization in surgery. When Don Giovanni, Letizia's father, discovered their relationship, he said to his daughter, "You want to marry him? Then go ahead, marry him. But I'm warning you, that man will drive you crazy!"

Her family's estate was in Monterosso, in the Siculiana countryside. It had all the charm of the great Sicilian estates of yesteryear; horses, stables, vineyards, olive orchards, a long dusty drive to the main house. The balconies were left open to encourage any breath of wind to come in, lace curtains fluttering like fans to placate the summer heat. Her parents, Alba and Giovanni, always had sweat on their foreheads. There was something tired in their faces, and sometimes they would shake their heads to dislodge flies that had touched down on the beads of sweat. Giovanni had blue blood in his veins; he was a descendant of the noble Antinori family. His aunt, Carmelina Antinori, would come to stay at Monterosso, her pearls and chignon giving her an old-fashioned air, while her fragrance of powder and talc added to her late-nineteenth-century demeanor. Carmelina had a trunk filled with antique hand-embroidered linens and silk sheets. One day, she gave part of her wedding trousseau to little Eleonora for her to use when she got married.

Giovanni was a lackadaisical man who would spit effusively in all directions on any occasion. However, he possessed an innate elegance he displayed with his Borsalino hats and the expensive walking sticks he collected. They were not required for support; his use of them was simply an affectation. He was an envious man, so strongly possessive of his wife that, when she leaned from the house's balcony, he shouted at her, "Go back inside; everyone down here can see your legs." He worried that the farmhands would look at Alba from the fields and imagine her naked limbs. Alba was sixty-five, her husband seventy years old.

Giovanni did not like working, but he loved the land he had inherited and ensured that the laborers always maintained the fields properly. When his friend, Don Ciccio Bellomo, would ask, "Don Giovà, how are you keeping?" Giovanni would reply "Good, as long as the weather keeps up." He would then move on to a discussion of women, during which he liked to make sweeping statements, such as, "Don Ci', women are more evil than men!" Don Giovanni enjoyed following the slow movement of the clouds. From his study of them, he was able to tell ahead of time when the rain would arrive. He longed for rain, which would nourish the vines and produce better wine.

Alba was a discreet and unpretentious woman. Against the odds and WWII, she graduated with a degree in literature from the University of Messina. She later recounted the story. "Back then, during the war, it was dangerous to cross Sicily by train with all that bombing going on. It was risking one's life." Her elegant and poetic expressions were in contrast to the boorish manners of Giovanni. Despite their differences, however, they were extremely fond of each other and did everything together, united as mind and body. When they were still newlyweds, Alba accompanied Giovanni to all his driving lessons so that if he did not understand some part, she would be able to explain it to him later. Once at home, she made him repeat the lesson to prepare for the final test. Alba never got her driving license, however. Giovanni learned how to drive, but did not drive well unless his wife was at his side. "Giovà, go into first gear, we're on a hill," she would remind him. "Stop here at the stop sign and turn right. No, right! That's left." And he followed her instructions.

The Carrubba family spent half the year in Monterosso— from spring to the autumn grape harvest. Eleonora had taken part in the ritual of the grape harvest from the age of three. She picked the mature grapes like her grandfather had showed her, and later crushed them with her little feet to obtain the juice. At day's end, Giovanni and Eleonora had fun washing in the basins filled from great water barrels. There were no water pipes in the countryside, where time had stopped at the previous century and a shower was considered a luxury. Grandmother Alba always reminded Eleonora that water was precious due to its scarcity, and she should always be careful not to waste any.

PERSEPHONE

In the farmhouse barn used as a garage was a red 1950s Porsche. The barn must have once been a stable; the sickly smell of horse manure still pervaded the air. The car belonged to Letizia's brother Ferdinando, and she was allowed the use of it whenever she liked. When Letizia decided to go for a spin, she put her daughter on her lap and they would zoom across the countryside and along the coast, their four hands on the wheel. People watched the car fly by with great curiosity, and Eleonora enjoyed waving at them from the window.

One day they drove as far as Agrigento. They stopped at the Valley of the Temples, got out of the car, and sat down at the Temple of Concord. In that windy valley, Letizia began to tell her daughter about the ancient Greeks, how they built their temples, their instinct for finding panoramic sites and how they chose the settings for their temples, their strategy to keep the enemy under control so they could attack at the right moment. Letizia knew all the Greek legends; Alba had told them to her from childhood in the very same place where

Letizia was now passing them onto her daughter.

Eleonora's favorite was the story of Persephone. "The maiden goddess," explained Letizia, "spent six months on Earth in Sicily with her mother Demeter, goddess of the harvest. For those six months, Demeter was so jubilant because Persephone was with her that she brought an abundance of flowers and fruit to the land with the flowering of spring and summer. When Persephone was forced to return to her husband Hades, King of the Underworld, for the rest of the year, Demeter showed her sadness at their separation by repressing the crops of the fields. Leaves would abandon their trees and the sky would fill with clouds."

In Eleonora's imagination, Persephone had appeared from the underworld into the concave valley she was admiring from above. They sat in silence until sunset, breathing in the energy of that place filled with ancient lives, and then got in the car and headed back to Monterosso. That day, Eleonora had asked her mother, "Why does Papa not want us to live at the farmhouse with Grandmother and Grandfather? It's so beautiful and so big. We could be like Persephone, who spends six months with her family." Letizia didn't answer but concentrated on driving, her sense of freedom now only tenuous.

Luigi was waiting for them at Monterosso, his expression furious. He had come to fetch them, his silence enough to ensure that they received their daily dose of guilt. With a nod of the head, he indicated to Letizia and his daughter that they should get out of the Porsche and into his car. Eleonora could only wave goodbye to her grandparents from a distance. They were silent in the car; no one talked, and there was no music, only several sighs. Luigi drove to a hill which rose steeply above the sea and told them, "This here is ours; it is our land, the most expensive in all the region. I will build a great villa here to be our house; it will be the best in the area."

"I don't want this land. I like the farmhouse," retorted Eleonora, "There are horses. Everyone loves us there." Her father answered, "Our house will be our home forever. No one needs to give us anything. When you are older you will realize that you need to make everything for yourself, with your own hands."

Letizia was proud of her husband; she gently placed a hand on his leg while she looked curiously at the newly conquered hill. Luigi held her hand in his, stared into her eyes, and kissed her on the mouth. They got out of the car to enjoy the celestial surroundings . The blue sky merged into the indigo sea on the horizon . *If the Greeks had seen this hill*, imagined Eleonora, *they would have built a temple here*. She inspected the place proudly while her parents chatted together.

"This is the site where I will build Villa Letizia," whispered Luigi in his wife's ear. "Now it's your turn to give me a present. I want a son." When they got back to the car, Luigi added, "There will be no reason for you to spend time at Monterosso; you will have everything you need right here."

FAVA BEAN SOUP

They drove to Villino Maddalena, where Grandmother Maddalena was waiting for them. She had made dinner, a Sicilian speciality—*macco di fave secche*, a soup of dried white fava beans simmered in very little water over a low flame for hours. A garnish of wild fennel, added before serving, was the perfect accent for the steaming cream soup.

After Eleonora's birth, her paternal grandmother had come to live with them. This had been decided by Luigi, who judged his wife incapable of handling the housework and was sure Maddalena could teach her. Letizia always addressed her mother-in-law as *Donna* Maddalena,[3] out of respect. When her son was away attending medical conferences, Maddalena was always quick to tell him if his wife had gone out "painted and dressed up," and informed him of Letizia's every movement, from turning on the hot water boiler to going to play cards with her girlfriends, without telling him. From her

---

[3] "Donna" or "Lady," is a respectful form of address for older women or those of noble background.

place in the armchair, dripping in make-up and jewelry, she watched Letizia constantly, her big green eyes in continual judgment. If Letizia looked sad after an argument with Luigi, Maddalena was always quick to reproach her. "It's your fault! You don't know how to treat my son properly. He's a good man, so good-hearted and such a good example."

Grandmother Maddalena would take Eleonora with her to gather capers or figs in the countryside, taking advantage of her granddaughter's small, nimble body to send her up fig trees to fetch the fruit. Luigi loved the countryside; he took great care of the fruit trees in the garden, which he watered often. It was a passion of his, and looking after the garden was how he relaxed after the day's work. Every year at harvest time, Maddalena told her granddaughter the same story, which began, "You must always respect and love your father. Look at the house he is building for you! You couldn't even begin to imagine the conditions in which we used to sleep. There was famine and war, and we had nothing. But your father, my son, decided that he wanted to be a doctor and make his dream come true—to have the most impressive house in the town."

The next day was Eleonora's first day at school. She was not yet five and could not write or read, but her father had decided that starting her education a year early would be to her advantage in the future. The school courtyard was filled with children holding hands with their mothers. Their white smocks had blue or pink bows. Eleonora had chosen a school bag with her favorite cartoon character, Candy Candy, on it.

Letizia spotted Eleonora's new teacher in the crowd. "Ms. Sinatra!" she cried, short of breath as she pushed her way through, pulling Eleonora behind her. "Ms. Sinatra, I entrust you with Eleonora. She has a few problems. Please keep an eye on her and pay her special attention." Eleonora had never realized that she had "a few problems" before. So while she stared resentfully at her mother for confiding such private information to a total stranger, she also began to consider the fact that if her mother thought this, it must be true. In the class, she played the role of the "child with problems." Of course, that meant no studying or doing well at school, so she didn't do either.

THE DRUM KIT

Eleonora had curly black hair that had grown too long for her father's taste. It was the day of her sixth birthday when Luigi took her to his barber, put her on the stool in the salon, and told the barber to cut her hair short, like a boy's. Eleonora watched the little curls float to the floor. The mirror reflected her father's severe expression. She tried to wriggle away—she couldn't keep still, she screamed and shouted, but he won out. Her eyes were sad; she felt deprived of a part of herself.

They returned to the little house on the beach. Letizia had organized a party for her daughter's birthday. Her cousins, uncles, aunts, and grandparents were there to welcome her with smiles, presents, and cameras. Luigi put a large package in her hands, which she opened to find a train set inside. When everyone gathered around the table and her cake and started singing "Happy Birthday Eleonora," Letizia became tearful, crying with emotion. Luigi rushed to bring the party to an end. After the cake had been cut and eaten, the guests gradually began to leave.

The child shut herself in her bedroom, an empty, white room that looked like the wards in the hospital where her father worked. There were many toys in there, but not a single doll. Balls, model motorcycles, a remote-control car, but no dolls. Aunt Laura, Letizia's sister, had given her a red drum kit, and it was gorgeous. She started to play it. Laura knew that Eleonora would enjoy the drums because she had watched her arrange rows of different-sized pans and lids and beat them with sticks hundreds of times as she tried to pick out the rhythm of the melodies, singing "*Sciuri Sciuri*."[4] She was sure that a real drum kit would be the best birthday present she could give her niece.

Eleonora taught herself to play, and drumming became her passion. The silence that had characterized Villino Maddalena and the slow rhythm of their days were now punctuated by the deafening beats Eleonora produced from her drum kit. But she was not allowed to play while her father was sleeping or receiving patients.

One room in the house was set up for use as a doctor's surgery, and when he wasn't at the hospital, Luigi spent a great deal of his time there. He was happy in that room and should never have left it. Sick and suffering children often arrived with their worried mothers. Luigi was good with

---

[4] A well-known Sicilian folk song.

them, knowing how to handle them so that they would all calm down and stop crying. He never allowed the poorest families to pay for their appointments and often gave them expensive medicines for free, along with some sweets.

Eleonora once pretended to have a bad headache and went into his study, asking to be examined like the other children. "What are you saying?" he asked. "You are strong and healthy. Go tell your mother. Can't you see I'm working?" Eleonora closed the door and found her mother in the garden, where she was sneaking a cigarette. Luigi was hot on her heels and caught Letizia in the act. He slapped her, grinding the cigarette into the grass. "You are to do what I tell you. You are not to decide by yourself because you always do the wrong thing! You cannot smoke; men smoke." Her lip was bleeding. They stared at each other. He dabbed the blood with his handkerchief. Without apologizing, he embraced her, making her breathless. Letizia let herself go. They kissed, biting each other, tightly entwined. He took her hand, and they went into their bedroom and closed the door.

Eleonora went to play her drums.

PHLEGM

Ms. Sinatra was not particularly fond of Eleonora, nor had she ever paid her the special attention that had been requested due to her "problems." Actually, she had never really noticed her in any way at all. Eleonora was simply parked in the class and left to her own devices. When Luigi was informed by the teacher that his daughter was on the lazy side, he decided that she should spend the next school year at Grandmother Alba's winter home in Agrigento. Perhaps the help of her teacher-grandmother would be a useful remedy.

Eleonora was six when she moved to the city. Her grandparents welcomed her with love, and Aunt Laura was enthusiastic that she had come to live with them. At her new school, Pirandello, the smocks were blue for both boys and girls. Every morning, Grandmother Alba would take her to Ms. Egle's classroom on the first floor, and then continue on to her own classroom on the second floor where she taught the last year of elementary school. Eleonora quickly learned how to read and write; her grandmother was brilliant with her after-school sessions. They would sit together at the blue table with steel feet and pull out notebooks and pencils from her school bag. Eleonora liked writing the letter *a* because it was round, but also rebellious with that little curl on the top. Her grandfather would sit with them and follow the lessons between phlegmy spits into his handkerchief. He hadn't studied much when he was younger.

Eleonora shared a bedroom with Aunt Laura, sleeping in the bed that had belonged to Uncle Ferdinando before he moved to Padua. One summer he had got his Paduan girlfriend Claudia pregnant and, to repair the damage, had married her. They were now a happy and content family with their children, Gianluca and Patrizia. Aunt Laura read every night before falling asleep, so Eleonora too picked up a book, keeping a covert eye on her aunt. When Laura turned the page, she would too. She had to learn the time it took to read each page, she thought, and could not understand how her aunt could be so quick when it took her such a long time to read one sentence, especially if there was an *s* or a *c* with an *h*, or the *s-t-r* combination. How long it would take to read a whole page!

Aunt Laura had a boyfriend named Salvatore, a good-looking boy. She was madly in love and planning to get married, have children, and live happily ever after. Salvatore, however, was a lover of women, and during their first years together, Laura had to battle her way to claim her place as his girlfriend—as the favorite one. Eleonora's grandparents never allowed Laura to go out with Salvatore alone for fear that she might lose her virginity before she was married. To appease them, Eleonora often accompanied the couple. Once, in a supermarket, while her aunt was busy checking produce labels, Salvatore was busy ogling the behinds of the other girls pushing their trolleys. Salvatore correctly read the look in Eleonora's eyes, which clearly said "dirty beast," and glared back at her, warning, "If you tell your aunt, I'll kill you."

Laura often told her niece to grow up fast so she could look after her children, Eleonora's cousins-to-be, when they were born. Laura once told Salvatore, in front of Eleonora, "Even if we have daughters, I'd still give Eleonora some jewelry. I love her like a daughter." Salvatore didn't reply, but glared at her. Laura rebutted, "Why shouldn't I? Anyway, it won't be for you to decide."

Some days later, though, her aunt's approach towards Eleonora changed drastically. She no longer confided in her or talked about her future.

This was the first feeling of betrayal Eleonora had experienced in her life. She couldn't believe that her adored aunt no longer loved her, but she felt it. It was, really, the second betrayal; the separation from her parents had been devastating. Eleonora would wait all week for two o'clock on Friday to come around. She stood on the balcony starting at one o'clock in her red overcoat and blue hat, waiting for her father's Renault 5 to appear on the horizon to take her home, but it was only for the weekend. Every Sunday evening, Eleonora would feel that mixture of infinite solitude and anger at her parents when they returned her to her grandparents' home.

LONG, LONG HAIR

Luigi and Letizia usually spent Saturday evenings at friends' houses while Eleonora stayed at home with her grandmother Maddalena. The women would talk among themselves about their latest purchases and sometimes play cards or gossip about those who were not present. Luigi went off with the men to play poker. They were serious players, and the stakes were always high. He would always stake his claim before going out for the evening. "Tonight I'm going to win" he would say, happy as a child, or "I'd better lose this evening or no one will want to play with me any more." It was all strategy. He knew perfectly well which tactics made his opponents nervous, and he won everything he wanted. If those who lost were businessmen, Luigi's winnings were sometimes paid in merchandise.

And so it was that mother and daughter happily approached the biggest clothing shop in the town, ready to pick up his winnings in kind. Mr. Cardella greeted them with a big, fake smile as they sacked the shop and went home without having to pay; the amount owed would be deducted from the gaming debt.

Once home, Eleonora went into her room, took her new clothes out from the shopping bags, and tried them on, striking model poses as she looked in the mirror. When she couldn't bear the sight of her short hair, she folded the crocheted tablecloth from her nightstand and used it as a wig, imagining that she had long, long hair. Her mother also put on her new outfit and came to her room to ask, "What do you think?"

"Fantastic," Eleonora would answer. "What about mine?"

"You look gorgeous, but I would cut that hair a little." Then they burst out laughing.

THE PERFECT FAMILY

On Sunday mornings, the Calabrò family would go to mass at the Church of San Gerlando. Eleonora sat between her parents, all dressed in their Sunday best, and after mass they usually went to buy *cannoli*[5] at the bar on Via Atenea. They couldn't go three steps without being called to in greeting. "Let me kiss your hand, doctor! Yours and your family's!" People stopped to acknowledge and compliment them. Even if husband and wife had argued ferociously the day before, Letizia was adept at disguising her bruises with makeup and hiding behind her smiles. Outside their house, they appeared to be a well-suited couple, the perfect family. "A devil at home, charming on the street," Letizia would say to her husband, remarking on the difference between Luigi's turbulence with his family and his good nature with other people.

One Sunday, Luigi took Eleonora out for a drive after

---

[5] The quintessential Sicilian pastries—tubes of fried dough stuffed with sweet ricotta

lunch. "You are going to meet some children who are not as fortunate as you," he said. Eleonora was happy to spend an entire afternoon with her father and to have him all to herself. Out in the countryside, they drove down dirt tracks, dogs running and playing alongside the car, until they came to a large farm. When they parked in the forecourt, children suddenly appeared, dozens of them, pouring out like ants from every direction. They were dark-skinned, wearing singlets and shorts, some of them bare-chested. The little girls looked just like the little boys with hair even shorter than hers. They appeared to recognize the car. Luigi opened the trunk and pulled out bedcovers, clothes, bags of candy, medicines, and all sorts of other things. The adults in their ragged clothes stopped their work on the land or with the animals and approached, removing their hats in respect and bowing their heads. They stood to one side, their eyes shining, sending the children up.

Only one woman came closer; she was pregnant. "Doctor, they should make you a saint!" she said and placed his hand on her belly. "If this is a boy, I want to name him after you. Luigi, I want to call him. Will you allow me to do that?" Luigi gave a half-smile with the right side of his mouth and shook her hand. Then he checked that they had taken everything from the car, closed the trunk, and said goodbye. Father and daughter set off. The smallest children followed them for a while, running behind the car and waving. On the journey back, Eleonora asked her father, "Do you buy the presents for the children from the money you win at poker?" He didn't answer; he just winked at her.

FULL MOON

Villa Letizia was finished. Built from rock and stone, it stood in the midst of the greenest hill in Agrigento, encircled by cacti and olive, orange, lemon, and palm trees. It ranged out to where the cliffs began, so close to the sea that the reflections on the water and the horizon seemed almost a part of the house.

That fall, a housewarming party was held at the villa. Flaming torches, a full moon, the silvery sea. Hundreds of people arrived in their cars with their drivers. It was like a film; the guests were beautiful and elegantly dressed, laughing happily, with Luigi and Letizia the most gorgeous of all. Husband and wife were kept busy looking after their guests and making a good impression, but from different sides of the room, they often stared into each other's eyes.

They made sure that the waiters were serving their guests with care. Long tables had been set up for the party on the patios surrounding the villa, groaning with a thousand delicacies—oysters winking on silver trays; lobsters on a bed of lemon slices garnished with curls of mayonnaise; steaming, fragrant *caponata*[6] decorated with mint and gladioli; hot potato sticks in straw baskets. The most impressive sight of all was the little Sicilian cart painted with scenes from the *Opera dei Pupi*,[7] brimming over with *panelle*! Panelle! Those irresistible little fried squares of chickpea flour! The history of panelle traces back to times of war. At first they were cooked mostly by the poorest of families, but over time had become a refined specialty that the wealthy could not resist. The guests competed to see who could eat the most. The crowning glory, however, was the ice cream cart that Luigi had rented for the evening. It was the very same cart that crossed the beach every day selling ice cream to the children, entirely hand-painted with pictures of giant ice cream cones and mermaids on a very, very blue sea. Parked for the evening in the garden, by the entrance gates, the vendor served ice cream, cannoli, and Sicilian *cassata*[8] through the side window hatch. A long line of people formed here too, queuing patiently as their eyes lit

---

[6] A sweet-and-sour eggplant dish with capers.

[7] Opera of the Puppets (Òpira rî pupi) is a marionette theatrical representation of Frankish romantic poems, such as The Song of Roland or Orlando furioso, that is one of the characteristic cultural traditions of Sicily. The opera of the puppets and the Sicilian tradition of cantastorî (singers of tales) are rooted in the Provençal troubadour tradition in Sicily during the reign of Frederick II, Holy Roman Emperor, in the first half of the thirteenth century.

[8] A traditional Sicilian cake made with sweetened ricotta, sponge, candied fruit, and almond paste.

up with the same anticipation that the thought of ice cream produces in children.

That night, Luigi lead the guests on a tour of the house. He proudly showed off the expensive marble, the precious Murano lamps, and the Persian carpets. Eleonora happily joined the group following her father, but soon she heard some of the guests deriding their host's delusions of grandeur. Ashamed, she ran off. When the tour had finished and everyone had gone out into the garden, Eleonora took a screwdriver and made a scrape on the inlaid table in the drawing room. The record player was playing the songs of Gino Paoli and Mina, and several couples were dancing to the slow music, renewing their promises of love. Past midnight, the guests gradually began to leave. They thanked Letizia for her warm welcome, praising the attention and care she had paid to every detail of the evening. She had been a wonderful hostess.

Luigi sent his daughter to brush her teeth before bed. He began to turn off the lights and the heating and lock up several of the reception rooms, which he said were only for special occasions and not needed. It didn't take him long to notice the scrape on the table. He called for his wife, still in her evening dress, and accused her of not keeping a sufficiently vigilant eye on the guests during the party, his rage growing until he slapped her. Eleonora watched the scene undetected. She shut her bedroom door, waited for the silence of the night, and then opened her window and crept out. She ran to the foot of the Turkish Steps, climbed the rock and, on the top, began to scream with all her might at the sea. The white rock shone pale in the light of the full moon. She screamed as loudly as she could and, spinning round and round in a dizzying whirl, fell exhausted onto the pure white ground.

SUMMER HOLIDAYS

Villino Maddalena had become the holiday home for the Calabrò siblings . Every summer , relatives arrive in Azur Beach from Palermo . Pino, Luigi 's brother , a brigadier in the Carabinieri , with his wife Sara and their children Ferruccio and Diana , took the ground floor, while the eldest sibling Gina, took the first floor. With the help of her mother Maddalena , Gina had managed to marry an army general . This was a coup , a rich and successful marriage . General Antonio Chiara 's work often meant the family had to travel from city to city wherever his presence was necessary , but they still managed to spend the summer

months at the seaside . Nino and Gina had four children ; Maddalena jr, Dario , Calogero , and Danila , each born in a different city.

During the summer, Villino Maddalena vibrated with the energy of its occupants and the peculiar characteristics that only grandparents' homes seem to have. Eleonora happily played hide and seek with her cousins, and as she knew every nook and cranny of the house, it was always very hard to find her—she was the best at secret hiding places. Ferruccio was Luigi's favorite nephew, their shared surname a point of union, and they spent a lot of time together. They organized informal football tournaments on the beach below the house that ended only when forced by sunset. Dario and Calogero played and other beach goers would join in while the women cheered from their sun loungers. Eleonora loved swimming at that time of day. The water was warmer then, when the golden sun had begun to melt into the sea, than it was in the morning. She would swim parallel to the shore in that shining strip of light, hearing the sound of applause in the distance when goals were scored.

Ferruccio often came to Villa Letizia to play ping-pong, billiards, or tennis with his Uncle Luigi. Ferruccio knew how to get on with him. Luigi gave him a Vespa 50cc scooter for his fifteenth birthday, and a gleaming new BMW for his eighteenth.

AN ANGEL FALLEN FROM THE SKY

Nine months after the tornado, Alessandro was born. Luigi and Eleonora went to visit in the hospital. "Hello Alessandro," said Eleonora through the glass. She watched the little body screaming and waving its legs and arms with a slight smile on her face. "He's the perfect son," said Luigi to his work friends, who congratulated him.

Letizia and Alessandro came home a couple of days later, and Villa Letizia became a thoroughfare of relatives and friends coming and going, congratulating Luigi and Letizia on the birth of their son. The uncles and cousins from Palermo appeared, thrilled with the arrival of another child in the family. The only exception to the shared joy was Ferruccio, whose expression appeared a little downcast. However, when Uncle Luigi approached, his face lit up in a cheeky smile.

Luigi gave Letizia a piece of expensive jewelry.

He would even wake several times in the night to check on Alessandro in his cot to make sure he was breathing. They were happy.

On his return from a work trip, Luigi finally brought a doll for his daughter, but he continued to take her to his barber for her hair. "Your hair is too curly; it makes your head look big," he said. Eleonora hated these trips to the barber, hated being forced to submit to an act of injustice that continued regularly until she turned fourteen.

Alessandro grew happily. With his blonde curls and big blue eyes, "he looks like a Norman warrior," Maddalena said. When Eleonora played her drums in the playroom, Alessandro would scurry over on all fours, indicating that he wanted to sit in her place, a big smile on his face. Eleonora would lift him onto the stool beside her and he would launch into incredible drumming sequences. He was decidedly better than she was, and soon their parents and cousins applauded his performances. He managed to attract everyone's attention when he played, adults and children alike. Eleonora was annoyed by his success.

Alex was almost two when he had his first epileptic seizure. He was playing the drums when Eleonora saw his face go black and, as he fell from the stool, she screamed, paralyzed by terror. Letizia ran in from the other room and bent over her son. Alessandro was drooling, eyes wide open and rolled back into his head, his whole body shaking, and a temperature of 104 degrees. She nursed her child without really knowing what to do. "Fetch some ice," she ordered her daughter. Eleonora ran off immediately. Long minutes passed before Alex completely returned to consciousness. "My love, how are you?" asked his mother. "*Es! Es!*"[9] replied Alex. She put him to bed in the room next door to his sister and stayed at his side until his father came home. When he was told about the episode, Luigi slapped Eleonora. "See what you've done? You have to let your brother do everything he wants. If he wants to play the drums, you mustn't be jealous." But she was not to blame; she hadn't shouted at him. She had only pushed him a little because he was throwing the drumsticks at her. "You are no longer my princess," he said. "Go to bed without dinner!"

In her bedroom, Eleonora put her ear to the wall to listen to her parents talking. Letizia was frightened by what had happened to Alex. "Why?" she asked repeatedly. Luigi spoke in a soft voice; she must be hugging him, thought Eleonora. "Alessandro was simply a little agitated. It was Eleonora's fault," said her father. "Nothing like this will ever happen again!"

Alessandro, however, was not yet talking; he could say less than ten words, and those in a way that was only decipherable to his family. Grandmother Maddalena consoled herself by saying, "Boys talk later than girls!" But his behavior

---

[9] "Yes. Fine."

was also out of the norm; he was always staring into the distance, absent. He would run off on his own, hide behind the armchairs in the house, and stare into the light bulbs or neon lights. He would rock in repetitive movements, and if anyone spoke in a loud voice or argued, he became very tense and started to shake. Luigi was not particularly worried by these aspects of Alex's behavior; when his wife pointed out the strangeness of it all, he answered "And so what? Are you the doctor now? You should just concentrate on being a good mother. You still don't know how to do that."

Without telling her husband, Letizia decided to take Alex to a specialist. Her daughter went too. The plate on the door was engraved "Doctor Carlo Albanese, pediatric neuropsychiatry." They went into his surgery. Eleonora immediately recognized him as a friend of her father's, a man who often lost to him at poker. Letizia gathered her courage and explained the difficulties that her son was having in speaking, adding that when he wanted something he had to point a finger, and that he had already had three epileptic fits. The specialist reassured her, "Don't be so dramatic. Sooner or later, the boy will bloom. Let's wait until he is five." She smiled and begged him not to tell her husband about the consultation.

But back home, Luigi was already in a raging fury; the doctor had betrayed her trust. "How dare you do that," he shouted at her. "My son is healthy, and you are mad!"

Eleonora was supposed to be in bed, but she was watching everything from the staircase. Luigi raised his hands, landing his fist on Letizia's face. She should have run away, far away, from him, but the next day she was still there in that house, shut in her room. Luigi went out early; Alex was still asleep. Before going to school, Eleonora knocked on her mother's door, which was open. Letizia had flopped on the bed; there were pills on the pillow, an empty bottle. Eleonora woke her grandmother, who telephoned Aunt Laura and her mother's cousins, Silvana, Gisella, and Ornella, her best friends since childhood, who all came to the house. Letizia was still alive; they made her vomit and took her to hospital.

Eleonora stayed at home with Alessandro and Grandmother Maddalena. That evening, she was finally allowed to see her mother. Before she went into her mother's room, Luigi warned her, "If anyone asks—here in the hospital, at school or your friends—your mother is here because she had appendicitis. Appendicitis. Is that clear?"

Eleonora didn't reply; she just glared into his eyes. He pushed her into the room. Letizia was alone, an IV drip in her arm. Pale, she managed a slight smile. Luigi said to her, with vehemence, "Don't ever try that again, especially in front of Eleonora. I swear, I'll take your children and I'll have you locked up. You know I can do that."

WALLS THE COLOR OF OCHRE

At the age which immediately precedes adolescence while also being its precursor, Eleonora created a parallel world for herself, a world all her own that was in total contrast to the real world, with which it would never come into contact. In her world, she allowed herself everything she wanted, making it a space where her dreams could flow and her wishes be expressed. Using homework as an excuse, she would shut herself in her room in a solitude warmed only by walls the color of ochre. She would stand in front of the double mirror of her wardrobe. Dressed as a ballerina, she would dance; at times, she would wear her Sunday clothes and pose as if the mirror were a camera, admiring the changes in her body as it became more sinuous and feminine.

In this world of hers, her favorite activity of all was drawing charcoal sketches of imaginative clothing . At times she would draw evening dresses, which called to be brought to life. She loved drawing her models onto big sheets of paper and, using scraps of material from her grandmother's trunk, making the clothes. Maddalena had taught her to sew and would correct the hems for her later. She would also judge the clothes, giving Eleonora points for each piece, pushing her to improve when she saw mistakes in her sewing. Her grandmother was proud of Eleonora, although she would not show it. She was not affectionate; she pointed out defects and hardly ever gave praise. "Children should be kissed at night when they don't know, or else they will grow up spoiled," she said. Eleonora's room was beginning to resemble an atelier in miniature with an ever-increasing number of drawings pinned to the wall, and clothes draped on the mannequins she had obtained from Mr. Cardella. He had agreed to give the shop's old ones to Eleonora when the new window replacements arrived every year rather than throwing them away.

Another of her private activities in her parallel world in the room with ochre walls was to write in her diary, recording every sensation and every thought. She wrote about Luca, her first boyfriend, who lived in Canicattì. He was good-looking with big brown eyes, an uptipped nose, and white, white teeth. It wasn't easy for them to meet as the distance between their hometowns was considerable, and Luigi did everything possible to obstruct his daughter's outings. Luca was a gentle soul. They wrote each other beautiful love letters, filling the time between their occasional meetings in the square, when high-energy emotion made their eyes sparkle and fixed beaming smiles to their faces. They communicated with the romanticism of adolescents in love, their voices gentle and soft, metered by loving effusions. Their words were characterized by absolute superlatives with no middle ground and everything colored in strong shades.

Luca and his family spent the summer in Lido Rossello, which was very close to Lido Azzurro. They were part of the same group of friends. Eleonora was allowed to go out in the evenings if she was with her cousin Ferruccio. He picked her up on the Vespa that Luigi had given him. They would go to Bar La Baia on the coastal road, where the rest of the group gathered with their scooters. Eleonora would jump off Ferruccio's Vespa and climb onto Luca's.

The group had a wonderful time together, riding scooters down to the sea, exchanging first kisses between swims, spending evenings on the beach by the kiosk, dancing barefoot in the moonlight. After a midnight bonfire on the mid-summer holiday of *Ferragosto*,[10] Ferruccio took his cousin home. He stopped outside the villa gates and said, "This is the last night I cover for you. You've got to sort something else out. I don't want your father to find out; I'll lose his trust." Eleonora did not answer but became very sad,

---

[10] Italian national holiday on August 15.

knowing that without his support, Luigi would not allow her to go out. Her face strained, tears rolling down her face, she suddenly stretched out to embrace her cousin in search of consolation. But Ferruccio slipped away and drove off on his scooter without saying goodbye. Eleonora stopped crying, disappointed in Ferruccio.

Luca's parents were first cousins. Well aware of the dangers involved, they had decided to marry because they were in love and couldn't live apart. Their first born, Luca's sister, had Down's syndrome. Luigi knew about Luca's parents and his sister's needs because Ferruccio had told him, so he began a war from which there was no way out for Eleonora and Luca. "You can't have a boyfriend whose sister has Down's syndrome. You realize you could have sick children if you get married? I forbid you to see him."

"But I'm fourteen years old", said Eleonora. "How can you think that I already want to get married?"

"Exactly. You are too young. I don't want to say this again." The last time she saw Luca, she told him that she couldn't meet him any more because she couldn't get out of the house and was being watched. All she could do was stop seeing him. Luca answered, "Just know that I'll wait for you till we're sixty!"

Eleonora found solace in her ochre-colored room and the sweet memory of a love that had not fully blossomed. She vented her emotions in her diary. Her eyes full of tears, she wrote, "I was born in this place, but I won't die here." She hated her father's mentality, the provinciality of the place, the lack of respect for human beings and, even more, the lack of respect for women. "Men are premier league, women second or even third league," her father always said.

"What would people say?" was a concept that conditioned them all, whether they were inside or outside the house. It was like having a hidden camera constantly focused on the interior of their home, making everyone careful of their every move. There was always a member of the family who thought they had the right to walk into a room without knocking, or someone who would read diaries not their own. "Respect" was not considered. Eleonora felt distant from that place and that society; she didn't recognize herself in the local habits and behavior. She felt like a fish out of water when listening to her classmates' chatter. Instead, she imagined a future full of travel, people, and success, not the husbands and children they talked about. A feeling of uneasiness gripped Eleonora, and she felt that the time she spent in the parallel world of her room was vital to keep her alive.

When anyone asked her what she wanted to do when she grew up, she hesitated before answering because she had never seen anyone from her town do what she wanted to do. Her mother felt she had the right to answer in her place, to make herself feel important although she knew nothing of what was going through her daughter's mind. Strangely, however, when she said, "Ele knows exactly what she is going to do when she grows up but she doesn't want to tell us!" it was the truth. Eleonora was not yet ready to say that she wanted to be a fashion designer. At times, though, she would question her ambitions, wondering, *If Mamma is convinced I can see my future clearly, why did she say I had "a few problems"?*

THE HAUNTED HOUSE

Eleonora also wrote in her diary about her classmates at middle school, in appreciation of their long blond hair and trendy clothes. Eleonora had started to grow her hair, but her knee-length socks and knee-length skirts embarrassed her. Her father would not allow her to wear fashionable clothes, saying that girls in miniskirts were only trying to get the boys' attention.

In her room, the silence of her thoughts was accompanied by the gentle sound of waves breaking on the rocks. It was the soundtrack of her dreams and the lullaby of her nights. There wasn't only the sea outside her window; close by was also the "haunted house." Sitting on the windowsill, she stared at it for hours, entranced, imagining countesses and baronesses in wide, white dresses strolling slowly through the gardens, their parasols protecting them from the sun, contemplating the blooms of spring flowers.

She often went there with Dario, her cousin from Palermo. It was an unfenced farmhouse with rows of ancient palm trees flanking the approach to the main door. It seemed that she could hear the sound of horses' hooves clattering, a carriage behind. The villa was in decay; parts of the roof had caved in, and it was dangerous but not difficult for their agile bodies to slip inside the door. The inner courtyard bore the date 1852 on a wall. They had fun searching every nook and cranny as if looking for hidden treasure. Perhaps there was something mysterious hidden beneath the splendid Sicilian ceramic tiles. *Who knows how many balls there must have been in these rooms, enveloped by these frescoed walls!* Eleonora thought, *Just like Angelica and Tancredi! How wonderful!* Within those tumbling walls, Eleonora and Dario begun to dance, humming the soundtrack from *The Leopard*. Smiling, Dario asked if he could kiss her. "Have you gone completely mad?" she answered and ran off towards the house. "There's nothing better than kissing your cousin," Dario sang out behind her.

"SORRY MIMI, ME MAKE MESS"

When Letizia had recovered her strength after the suicide attempt chronicled as appendicitis, she was sent home from the hospital. She returned as if nothing had happened—kind, submissive, remissive. However, she confided in Eleonora, "I came back for you, my children. Only for you." She attempted to wound her husband by letting herself go, but she was unable to become ugly. Luigi wanted her to be beautiful. Everything had to seem perfect to him and for "what people think." She was, in fact, still as beautiful as she had been when she was twenty.

Meanwhile, Alessandro's development had not progressed since he was three; he was now seven years old. His vocabulary was limited to non-conjugated verbs and the names of people and things. Eleonora tried to get him to sing her favorite songs by Renato Zero and Pooh into an air microphone. She would annunciate the words clearly for him to follow, but he simply responded with his smile and his habitual good humor. "Ale play drums, Mimi sing." His sister was Mimi to him; he didn't like the name Eleonora. So everyone began to call her Mimi.

He was a very lively child, full of joy for life, whose friendly charm made it possible for him to obtain everything he wanted. Physically, he was growing well. However, when he tried to express himself, he made sounds that resembled words, but were incomprehensible.

He would race around on his bicycle, careering across the countryside, not a care in the world and apparently free of any problems—his movements were completely normal and healthy. One day he fell off his bike. It was not a serious accident, just a few scratches on his knee, but Luigi noticed and threatened his wife. "If Alessandro goes out on his bike again, you will have to deal with me." On his own, Alex understood that if he wanted to protect his mother he should never ride a bicycle again, which is what he did.

Letizia encouraged him to develop his language abilities every day. After collecting the children from school, she would park outside the bakers' shop, hand a 1,000 lire banknote to Alex, and send him in. "Go ask for two bread rolls, and make sure you get the change." Then she waited anxiously in the car. He would return with a smile, proud of his accomplishment and, slipping happily into the passenger seat, basked in her congratulations, "Well done. Alex. You did brilliantly." There was nothing more precious than the "Tanks, Mummy," which came with a kiss for his mother, and "Tanks, Mimi," which came with a kiss for his sister. When the family went to the seaside, Letizia continued the system. "Alex, take this money, go to the bar on your own, and buy an ice cream. Buy one for Eleonora, too." He would show the barman the picture of two strawberry ices on the advertisement and ask, "'Scream, me, give me, two." He would come back to the beach, give one to his sister, and open his own. He ate it in a rush, keeping his eyes fixed on Eleonora's; he knew she would give it to him. He would eat lots of ice cream, one after the other, if only he could.

Back home, Letizia excitedly told her husband about Alex's progress at the bar and bakery. Luigi replied, "You know he doesn't speak properly. Someone is bound to tease him, and he would be mortified. Don't ever let him go out alone again." Letizia obeyed; she didn't want arguments at home. But she realized that Alex became particularly agitated when he picked up on a change of energy in the people around him, especially his family members, and he was disturbed when someone's voice got louder or the speed of their speech faster. Then he would have an attack—a crisis. He would throw anything he could get his hands on, shouting, "No, no, go 'way, Uncle Gigi, go." He often struck out at his mother, and it wasn't easy to hold him back, especially as he was growing so big and strong. He would fight her in an animal struggle, grabbing her arms, punching, biting, and kicking her legs. During his attacks, Alex's expression changed and his eyes become glassy, as if another entity had taken possession of his body, bent upon attacking and destroying everything in his sight—and generally his mother or his father was in his sight.

Letizia and Luigi suffered and feared, then became resigned that for the inexplicable rage which took possession of their son; there was a purpose hidden somewhere, they were serving a fault, invisible but vivid, that had to be expiated there, in that family, by Alexander. Only their souls knew exactly what game they were playing. The aggressiveness of Alexander, directed exclusively at his parents, had the taste of something that belonged to a distant time, to other past lives, an anger that seemed to want to equalize accounts still outstanding. It seemed incomprehensible to their minds, but necessary to conclude the effects of karmic causes triggered who knows how long ago.

In contrast, Eleonora had never feared her brother, knew Alexander would never hurt her, and would never have looked at her with hatred. Eleonora was only a helpless spectator within that dynamic. She remained to watch, motionless, like when you watch a play in which you are completely involved emotionally, but physically you cannot fight back, you cannot go on stage and decide to change the lines or actions because they are too full of suffering.

Alex referred to these crises as "the mess." They were becoming increasingly frequent, and were often precursors to epileptic fits. "Calm down, darling," Letizia would say with a sad expression. At the end of every fight, they would both be heartbroken and upset, raging with unexploded anger.

When Alex finally became himself again, he begged pardon. "Sorry Mamma, kiss, sorry Mimi, Grandma, sorry Uncle Gigi, me mess." Then he would make the sign of the cross and add "Sorry, Jesus. Dammit!"

These attacks were like a short circuit in his brain that allowed evil to take over his body. Alex would stare at his family with an expression that seemed to say, "I don't know what comes over me. It's got nothing to do with me!" The sweetness would return to his expression after the attacks, and everyone would stare at him, incredulous and stunned that the same body could host such contrasting elements—the joyful child and the devil.

Everyone in the family realized perfectly well that Alessandro had a serious problem, but no one wanted to broach the topic. Sometimes relatives or close friends would brazenly ask Letizia and Luigi, "Why don't you take this child to a specialist? Already eight years old and he can't talk properly." Luigi brushed off their concerns, replying that it would happen sooner or later. They tried to deflect the subject by staying in the joyful lightness of being that Alex created when he wasn't caught up in a mess.

Alessandro and Eleonora enjoyed playing together. She was very protective of her brother, accepting him as he was, with all his strangeness. They had invented their own way of communicating. When Alex raised his eyes to the ceiling and pointed upwards, he would say, "Look Mimi, an angel falling from the sky."

"Yes! True! See how many are over there!" she replied. They would imagine a whole host of dancing angels and slowly begin to dance, fully aware that they were teasing and egging each other on.

Eleonora imagined the angels to be transparent and smoky, and she wondered how Alessandro imagined them. What were his thoughts made of? He had a strong, unique personality that always attracted attention. Eleonora often observed her brother and reflected that he was the purest person she had ever known, without filters for his thoughts or attempts at pretense.

THE VENICE CARNIVAL

On Letizia's thirty-fifth birthday, Luigi appeared at the villa with a purple Golf Cabriolet for his wife. He knew her weakness for sports cars. "Pack your bags, we are going to celebrate in Venice!" Their eyes lit up; Eleonora loved traveling, Alex loved Carnival, and Letizia loved seeing her children happy. "Yes! Going me, car pretty!" exclaimed Alex. They set off in the new car.

When they arrived in Venice, the city was in full explosion of its celebration, happiness vibrating off every mask and every gondola. They sat down in a fancy restaurant for lunch. Eleonora was not very hungry and left some food on the plate. "You are to eat it all, right now," ordered Luigi. "Children in Africa die of hunger, and you leave food?"

Luigi grabbed Eleonora's arm. Letizia didn't try saying anything to protect her daughter, and tensions were rising. Alex began to show signs of agitation, trembling, his eyes contorting, until he exploded, throwing a plate to the floor. At the noise, the other clients in the restaurant turned in unison.

"It's nothing, nothing, our apologies," said Luigi "He'll calm down now and we will get out of here." But no one wanted them to leave; they all appeared to understand the situation.

Luigi decided to take his son to an old university colleague , a Venetian doctor who specialized in child neuropsychiatry . Two days of examinations , ECGs , and meticulous testing followed . The Venetian friend opened Luigi 's eyes . " The test results confirm Alessandro 's intellectual paucity and lack of language skills . I am sorry , Doctor."

"But he's perfect! Blonde, lively, attentive eyes. Some problems are only temporary; they'll disappear as he grows up."

"I am sorry, but you must know the truth. It is highly unlikely that Alessandro's problems will improve with time. Alessandro has autism; he will never speak fully." During the explanation, Alex laughed as he clicked a lamp on the professor's desk on and off, closing his eyes as it clicked off and opening them joyfully when the light was on. His father was furious, and as they left the doctor's office, he didn't even thank his colleague for his time.

They mingled with the carnival masks in the alleys of Venice. A tear slid down Letizia's cheek from behind her sunglasses. She was carrying her son, trying to buoy herself up. "We'll take him to other specialists—"

Her husband interrupted. "No, this is humiliation enough. He is healthy, and sooner or later he will be perfect."

Alessandro turned to Eleonora, waving his hands. "Lovely carnival Mimi, me carnival, buy confetti me?" Amid the general euphoria of the partying crowds, a street artist presented Alex with a balloon, smiling at him. Alex tried to wriggle out of his mother's arms, delighting in the festive atmosphere; he wanted to enjoy all the masks he could see around him. He suddenly let go of Letizia's hand and began sprinting, followed by Eleonora. To the crowd's surprise and his parents' horror, he came to a screeching halt at the edge of the canal. There he stretched his arms high into the air and tilted his head back to the sky, shouting, "Tanks, carnival, tanks." Then he began to dance in a circle, looking for other hands to bring in. His sister took his and they mingled together with the masked people, whirling around together, bringing Luigi and Letizia, shocked, into the dance.

"ME GO OUT, PIZZAURANT, CHRISTMAS"

Once back home, Eleonora ran to the Turkish Steps, to the highest point of the rock, rain thumping down around her. She screamed as loudly as she could and, spinning round and round in a dizzying whirl, fell exhausted onto the pure white ground.

At fifteen, she was too young to foresee the destructive effect the word "autism" would have on her life. However, she realized quite clearly that the word, heard for the first time in Venice, would totally change her life and the way she interacted with the world. It was as if her adolescence was suddenly interrupted and she had become a premature adult. Her brother was autistic. She didn't know what it meant, but it was obviously a disorder, an anomaly, that was never going to go away. When there is an autistic child in a family, the whole family is autistic, and Eleonora understood at a deep level what was going to happen later. That day in Venice, her connective tissue had been disturbed. *Will I be able to have healthy children one day?* she wondered. *What is autism?*

Villa Letizia soon became a prison as Luigi increasingly forced his family to isolate themselves in that gilded cage. It became obvious that he was embarrassed to be seen with his son and that he would not accept his illness, his difference. All that remained for his children was playing in the garden until Luigi sent them to rest every afternoon. He would send Alex inside saying, "Go straight away, brush your teeth." Then he would order Letizia to shut the windows and Eleonora to study in her bedroom.

His father's peremptory tone always made Alex jumpy. "No sleep, no, Uncle Gigi, no," and he would scream and struggle and run off into the garden, "Me go out, pizzaurant, Christmas, 'luminations, dums, steet stalls, party, merrygoround."[11] Letizia would follow him and try to calm him down, pulling him to her tightly while he struggled and punched and kicked, subjecting her to the entire gamut of his violent outburst. If that weren't enough, Luigi would stand there without defending her, repeating the same sentences. "It's your fault. You're no good at looking after him. You're useless. God is punishing you because you are a disgrace." They would wait for the attack to end; then the deepest silence descended and a heavy energy pervaded the atmosphere.

---

[11] "I want to go out, pizzaurant, Christmas, illuminations, drums, street stalls, party, merry-go-round."

AUTISM

Luigi researched autism. He read Letizia one of the first theories published in the sixties on the subject. The "Refrigerator Mother" hypothesis suggested that the problems of autistic children were related to emotionally cold mothers, who were unable to provide the support needed for their development. According to these studies, Luigi gathered, the autistic child creates the illusion that he is indivisible from the mother, whom he experiences as an offshoot of his body. To avoid separation anxiety, the child annuls his existence, living with, for, and in the mother, in sensorial and motor fusion with the maternal figure from whom it is difficult to be absent.

Luigi upheld the theory that it was essential to avoid any kind of change to create a quiet life for the autistic child; his reading indicated that modifying daily habits could upset the subject, who would become choleric, thus triggering an attack and its physical manifestations. As a result, he ordered that meals, games, sleep, clothing, and friendships follow a routine. His research also convinced him that if an autistic child, "incapable of thinking," were to spend time with children of his own age, he would inevitably become the object of derision. He was absolutely convinced that it would be "a cruel procedure, dressed as good practice." The cruelty lay in the lack of positive effect on the subject due to his mental immaturity, and in creating a heightened "hunger for the mother figure," a characteristic typical of almost all sufferers of autism.

It was that "almost" that made the difference. Alessandro was not like that. He loved being with people and, if permitted, would greet every passer-by. He didn't want to be with his mother all the time. On the contrary; Eleonora couldn't believe he could not make progress as he had these good traits; he was curious about life, and had he had support from experts and speech therapists, he could have made notable progress in autonomy and independence. Alex was so sociable, interested, and enthusiastic about life that his father could not believe this to be true of him. While it is true that autism manifests with different variants from sufferer to sufferer, and there are autistic children who do not enjoy socializing. It was obvious that Luigi had embraced theories that were not suitable for his son. These theories had been put forward over thirty years earlier and had been discredited or challenged by more modern scientific research.

Perhaps it was also that the Refrigerator Mother hypothesis was useful to Luigi; it established Letizia as the cause of their child's disorder. Luigi's approach appeared to be less about a search for the path to follow in the care and development of Alex's social, intellectual, and linguistic abilities, and more about imprisoning his wife in a way that would keep her in her place and under control.

Luigi also believed that therapists were totally useless. All that was needed for Alex was to ensure that he was looked after in every way at home, and that family members, in rotation, sacrificing their lives for love of him, would guarantee a continual presence. "After all," Luigi added, "I have provided this villa with a large range of games and sports. Occupations simply need to be organized with planned pauses for relaxation. This is why I am telling you three not to leave the house; you have everything you need here." These were the orders he gave. In his plan, this was all to fall on Letizia's shoulders. And, of course, Luigi did not include himself among those looking after Alessandro. He never missed a chance to insult Letizia, whom he called the "family disgrace." He accused her of "only being fit for wearing makeup, spending time aimlessly, and not knowing the first thing" about looking after her children.

ILLUMINATIONS AND LOCAL FESTIVITIES

Letizia's mission had always been to look after other people at the expense of her own life. That path appeared to have been marked for her when, as a child, she was sent by her father Giovanni to live with elderly, widowed Aunt Carmelina, to look after her in everything and to keep her company. As an adult, she was doing the same with Alessandro. She thought it normal to sacrifice herself for others, and never contemplated handing care of her child to other people or to an institute. Letizia did not find looking after the child a hardship, even without her husband's help. After Alex's very first epileptic fit at the age of two, she had left the marital bedroom to move into her son's to care for him at night. The child was not independent; his autism had caused continual gastrointestinal problems and a hiatal hernia, and he required assistance day and night. If he had been given the right treatment, with expert encouragement, from his earliest years, Alex would certainly have been able to learn how to wash and dress himself, to walk in the street, and to read and write. But nothing was done to further his development. Despite his suffering, Alesssandro was always smiling and cheerful. His joy and enthusiasm for life were amazing and contagious; he was always ready to joke with everyone.

Eleonora thought he was the most charming child on earth. He grew tall and increasingly handsome. His strongest characteristic was his ironic take on life. On meeting someone with a limp, he would mimic it, knowing that this would make his mother and sister laugh. When Carmelo, their deaf-and-dumb neighbor, visited, Alex imitated his alphabet, waving his hands around his mouth and emitting low, guttural sounds. Carmelo laughed; Alex knew how to go straight to people's hearts. He was a pure soul with no filters; he did not need them. Once, sitting in the passenger seat of the car next to his mother, he saw a car slow in overtaking them, so he opened the window and shouted at the driver, "Come on, go on, idiot." Unaware of the meaning, he simply knew it was an insult.

Letizia and Eleonora would hide their laughter. Alex, proud of himself, answered "Tanks, girls, tanks" in the voice of Pope John Paul II as he waved his hand in blessing, making the sign of the cross.

Alex had a method all his own for measuring the year. He wasn't interested in days or months in terms of seasons or climate; he followed his personal calendar of festivities and local feast days—Christmas, New Years, the Festival of Flowering Almond Trees in Agrigento, the Carnival in Sciacca, the Celebrations of May 3 in Siculiana, the Feast of St. Calogero in Porto Empedocle, and so on. He lived for this calendar. His father didn't stop him from going to the celebrations; it was the only concession allowed, and Luigi let them all leave the house. The local feast days had become important appointments not only to Alex, but to the whole family. Luigi recognized a separate world in the local celebrations, one where the attention was not on people but on symbols. Everything was altered by symbols, from the religious rituals to the urns with Christ's remains, from the statues of saints to the musical bands, from the carnival costumes to the festival's floats. Luigi was secretly convinced that, on these occasions, their family's "difference" was less obvious to people and would pass unobserved.

Alex loved the colorful lights, the bands, the street markets, the cotton candy, the processions with saints' statues carried on pilgrims' shoulders, and the fireworks. But most of all, he was fascinated by the illuminations. The first time that he saw those ropes of lights hanging between streetlamps and buildings, creating long bright arches in the night sky, he was enchanted. He was so struck by them that he talked about them every day, enthusiastically dubbing them simply "'Luminations!" When he repeated the word "'Luminations," he would elongate the vowels, hoping the sound would not come to an end while his eyes lit up, his eyebrows crept ever higher with wonder, and his mouth curled in a smile. His life had sense because it was tuned to the joy inherent in everything. For him, life was about laughing in happiness and enjoying the things that he liked; he knew no other ways of understanding existence. When he saw his father angry, his mother crying, or his sister sad, he said, "Lovely life, no bad you, all children laugh."

One spring afternoon, Alessandro, Letizia, and Eleonora went to the amusement park. Alex was an expert in Dodgem cars; he could slip past the others in the crush, and was good at bumping them when he wanted to. During his turns in the ring, he would get caught up in the music and colored lights and, rapt in excitement, would list all the swear words that his cousins had taught him at Monterosso—"'uck, shit, bitch, balls." The boys driving the other cars found him amusing and curious, and at the end of the round, one approached to Letizia to ask, "Signora, is your son from Romania?"

Letizia smiled as she answered, "Yes, we adopted him."

"Ah," said the boy, "that's why I didn't understand him properly!"

Returning home in the car, they were singing Pooh (Italian pop) songs when the wailing siren of an ambulance distracted them. The road was blocked at the height of an ancient, majestic palace; curious onlookers were running. They got out of the car. Alex slipped between the bystanders because he wanted to see what had happened, and he dragged them by the hand to the body of an elderly man crumpled on the ground. The injured man was having trouble breathing. Letizia was worried about Alex; she was not sure how he would react. He turned to face the windows of the palace and declared, "They throw grandpa, window. He old." Hoping that no one had heard, Letizia took Alex by the hand and walked off. But all had heard; she realized that from the stiff smiles of those around her. For Letizia, this was the first phrase of logical progression that her son had ever made. Excited, she decided to go to the hospital and find her husband to share her joy.

THE BASKET OF ORANGES

From a distance, Alex spotted Luigi on the ward, surrounded by doctors and nurses. He ran toward his father, his arms open, his smile wide, and exclaimed, "Uncle Gigi, Uncle Gigi, grandpa fallen!" He started to laugh, unable to stop, in a way that was infectious to all around him as Luigi stood unmoving. He couldn't bear that his son called him "Uncle Gigi." With his eyes cold and full of hate, he glared at Letizia, whispering through gritted teeth, "Take him away, go." They returned home, heads hanging low. Letizia was worried, certain that on his return home Luigi would make the mess, as Alex called it—explode. Every time he came back to himself after an attack, after the shouting, the kicking, and punching, Alex would look around and check his family's expressions, and as if in apology, say, "The mess me! Dammit!" Luigi came home that evening when all three were already asleep. The subject was never brought up again, and the mess was avoided that evening.

The next morning, Eleonora woke up early. Her father

had already left the house, and her mother was in the kitchen with a tiny woman, a farmworker, clearly poor but wearing her Sunday best, who had brought a basket of oranges as a gift. She was apologizing for disturbing Letizia and for the modesty of her offering. Eleonora recognized her as the pregnant lady in the countryside whom she had seen when her father had taken her to give gifts to the children. When the woman spotted Eleonora, she kissed her on the forehead and exclaimed, "How you've grown, little one!" Then she turned to Letizia, took her hand and, with a nod of her head, kissed it. She whispered with emotion, "Thank you, my lady. Yesterday your husband saved the life of my son Luigino. He had a bad heart; now he's better. He should be made a saint!"

From then on, Luigi became very fond of that unlucky but brave child who had fought alongside his surgeon to stay alive. Luigi invited him to Villa Letizia and taught him to play billiards and ping-pong. They often went fishing together. He also taught him to play tennis on the court at the villa while Alex and Eleonora sat on the terrace. Eleonora understood; Luigino was the son her father had always wanted. He didn't have money, but he went to school. Luigi supported his whole family. Letizia had also worked this out, but said nothing.

One day, Luigino was playing tennis with a friend at Villa Letizia. Alex and Eleonora were watching the game from the umpire's chair. "See?" said Eleonora to Alessandro, "We've got ourselves another brother. He has to go." With no further ado, Alex turned on the faucet attached to the hose and began to chase Luigino across the court, shouting at him "Go, go home you, go you," while soaking him from head to foot.

Eleonora was proud of her brother Alessandro.

CAKE IN THE FACE

On her seventeenth birthday, Eleonora's father invited Luigino to join them without first asking her. Luigino was not yet eleven. All Eleonora's classmates from high school were there. "Where does he fit in?" she murmured. Alessandro was happy, singing "Happy Birthday" and clapping. When he saw the cake, he got ready to blow out the candles with his sister as he did every year. Once the candles were out, Alessandro took the cake and shoved it in Luigino's face, just like in a slapstick comedy routine. Everyone laughed, except his father, who declared that the party was over. The guests left. Eleonora was so stunned that she couldn't even cry, even though she wanted to.

Luigi accused his daughter of instigating Alex against Luigino and took away all her gifts. He shouted at her and accused his wife of not knowing how to raise children. Alex, who couldn't bear the noise from all the chatter, fell prey to an attack. "No, Uncle Gigi, go 'way Uncle Gigi." He started to kick the gifts, glaring at his father in rage but venting his anger on his mother, punching and hurting her. Eleonora was shocked. Not only did her father not lift a finger to stop Alex from hitting his mother, but he also egged him on, saying, "Kill this disgrace of a woman, she's ruining our life!" Exhausted, Alex calmed down and stopped. His expression was disbelieving, as if to ask "Papa, how come? You encouraged me instead of stopping me?" Strained and in pain, he caressed the bruises and wounds he inflicted on his mother's face. "Me good me, good me. Mess me. 'Scuse me?" "Yes, my love, I know, you are a good boy," answered Letizia. "It's all over. Let's go to sleep now."

Once again the villa filled up with that life-sucking, heavy energy. Eleonora couldn't believe that her father's loathing of her mother had reached such a stage. She hated her father for the pain he brought them all, she felt responsible for protecting her mother, and she wanted to do something for her brother. She tried to encourage any development for Alessandro; there had to be a way to help him, a shred of hope for this disorder. She quickly realized that talking about it with her father was useless; his pain was stronger than the hope for recovery. Eleonora's unease kept growing.

"PAPA CRY"

One September afternoon, Eleonora was enjoying the sea breeze on the terrace, reading a book. Luigi was at work, and Letizia, before starting to clean the house, had asked her to keep an eye on her brother. He was on the swing, where he was capable of sitting for hours, going up and down, lulled by the steady rhythm. Eleonora decided to drive her mother's car around the villa garden; she enjoyed herself, slipping through the trees in an impromptu slalom. Alex watched her enthusiastically. Eleonora asked him, "Shall we go out for a spin?" He accepted eagerly. "'Esss, clever Mimi." They drove through the gate and headed off towards the city. Alex was always so happy when he was with his sister; he would have followed her to the end of the world.

Eleonora was sure that the police would not stop them. She felt like an adult, as if she already had her driving license. She had heard an announcement on the radio that Renato Zero would be holding a concert in Agrigento that evening, and she was determined not to deny this opportunity to her brother. Alex noticed the posters for the concert around the city and exclaimed, "'Ood God, Mimi, concert Renato Zero. Go you me?"

"Of course we're going! This evening, we're going to have fun," replied his sister.

"Tanks Mimi, fabulous."

They held hands at the stadium, happily running down to just below the stage. Going to a concert with Alex was great fun. Eleonora enjoyed herself watching him play air drums and imitating the drummer on stage. Suddenly, there was a hand on their shoulders. It was Letizia. The three of them stared at each other happily. Eleonora shouted at her, over the music, "Let's run away from him, just us three. Let's not go back home." Letizia squeezed her daughter's hand, crying as she sang along. At the end of the concert, tired but exhilarated, they headed to the car. This time Letizia drove. It was a silent journey, each lost in their own thoughts, their ears buzzing with the loud music. They returned home.

Luigi was sitting on the garden bench, ready to reproach them, but a trembling Letizia intervened first. "We had a great time at the concert! The three of us are always happy when we are together. You cannot keep us in prison." Luigi said nothing as Letizia kept her children close to her side, as if protecting them. Alex observed his father in the half light, then sketched a smile and said, "Papa, Papa is crying, Papa cry too." It was the first time he had called him Papa.

CHRISTMAS BAUBLES

Soon it was time for the Christmas festivities. This was the magical moment in Alex's festivity calendar. Every year, on December 8, the entire family followed the ritual. First, to Alex's great joy, they decorated the Christmas tree in the garden. Then two or three smaller trees were taken into the house to be placed where he wished. They enjoyed decorating the large fir tree with lights and hanging baubles of all types. Luigi bought large quantities of decorations, to his son's immense pleasure. Alex would stare at the lights in a trance and sing all the Christmas melodies in his own language-"*Tu scendi dalle stelle*," "Jingle Bells," and others. Luigi allowed him to keep the trees and the lights in the house even when Christmas was over. Alex wanted it to be Christmas all year long.

That day as they were decorating the fir in the garden, no one noticed Alex move away. He went over to his father's car, where he had spotted a red package. The car was open; he sat in the driver's seat and unwrapped the gift, but was distracted by the steering wheel. He started to steer, imitating his father, whom he had watched countless times. Then Alex turned the key in the lock and released the hand brake. The slight dip towards the sea helped speed up the car, which he weaved through the trees, using all his Dodgem experience.

Soon the car hit the railings, which were sent flying over the edge. The resounding thud caught everyone's attention. They all stood astonished, colored baubles in their hands, as the car flew through the air. Suspended for several seconds, Alex felt happy; he was flying through the sky like an angel. He had never felt anything this intense before! Then the car bumped to the ground, flipping over several times, skidding toward the cliff. It came to a halt upside down, a meter from the edge, wheels spinning, grey smoke belching, rocking. They all ran down to rescue him, the baubles rolling down the slope faster than they. "Keep calm, love," they shouted, "we're on our way."

Alex managed to get out of the car by himself. He was laughing in his own inimitable way. Feeling heroic, he punched the sky, a few minor wounds bleeding. "Greeattt, tanks, had fun me." Luigi turned to Letizia, furious. "What will happen to Alessandro when I am not alive?" Alessandro was still laughing and hugged his father. "Uncle Gigi, nothing happened me. Game car game."

The next day Letizia discovered the new plan that

her husband was scheming when Luigino's mother came to see her. "Donna Letizia," she said, "your husband, you probably know, gives us money so my son can study. He wants to be a doctor when he grows up, and your husband should be blessed for this. But yesterday he told us—me and my husband—that he will give us more money if we take care of Alessandro after his death. I need to ask for your forgiveness." She continued in tears, "This is not something we can accept. You are his mother."

Letizia sat there, not breathing, feeling totally empty. Alex hugged the tiny woman and said, "No cry you, it Christmas!"

FOR GRACE RECEIVED

After Alex's car accident, Luigi decided to make an offering to the priest holding the Christmas evening church service. "Father, this is in acknowledgement of grace received. It is a miracle my son is still alive," he said, and told him the story. The priest blessed the family, ruffled Alex's hair, and said goodbye with the sign of the cross.

After midnight, all four followed the procession of the live nativity and the musical band down the main street of the city, Via Atenea. Alessandro's eyes lit up; he slipped away from his father and ended up at the head of the band. He grabbed a drum from one of the musicians and launched into a solo that was perfectly timed to the melody the band was playing. The musical director, Sasà, let him finish and, with a tap of his baton, stopped Luigi from intervening. When Alessandro came to the end of his piece and elegantly handed the instrument back to its owner, a ripple of applause grew from the gathered throng who clapped for five minutes, their eyes full of admiration.

Due to the grace received, Luigi could not refuse Maestro Sasà's suggestion that Alex join the church's official marching band. And so Alex would greet the crowds, playing the drum during the festivities at the head of the band, next to Maestro Sasà. At the director's nod, he would launch into a solo. He loved to hear the crowd applaud and, when he did, he threw his drumsticks in the air, thrilled with the experience.

Over the next couple of months, Maestro Sasà fell ill. Accompanied by Letizia, Alessandro visited him at home with his drum to learn the band's repertory properly. "You're getting better and better," said Sasà. "Tank you Sasà, you my friend," answered Alessandro.

Sasà died one November morning, a tumor having reduced him to skin and bone. The entire population of the city was present at the funeral, and everyone felt very sad. Alessandro did not understand the idea of death nor the need to keep silent behind the casket. He had insisted on bringing his drum, and every now and again would give it a tap. He was extraordinarily in time with the soft footsteps of the mourners, who were silently smiling.

Sasà would have liked that funeral.

WILD FLOWERS

Eleonora's first trip away from home by herself was a well-deserved present for her high school graduation. It was organized by Rotaract, a youth program she did not belong to, although she had friends who did. She was invited to join them and Luigi agreed, deeming her friends good kids, many of whom were the children of his friends.

On that holiday, Eleonora met Giacomo, the travel agent who accompanied them. Ten years older than she, a tennis player and full of incredible energy, he was one of those people who could do anything they put their mind to. They immediately hit it off and talked their way through the tour. Giacomo talked much more than Eleonora, and realized that she wasn't used to chatting. "You will only truly understand who you are and what you want from life by talking a lot to people you trust," he told her. Across the Sila mountain range and through the villages of Calabria, he encouraged her to believe in the possibility of happiness and in the connection between dreams and reality.

That trip changed her outlook on life. Thanks to Giacomo's encouragement, she was able to clearly identify what she wanted to do with her life and, even more importantly, she realized that love is love, and it resembled nothing of what she was used to in her family—silence, rage, and hate.

It was not easy for her to return to the microcosm of her home after breathing the air of freedom, especially when Luigi read her private diaries, found out the details of her trip, and forbade her to leave the house. She was, however, no longer prepared to listen to him about what she should or shouldn't do. She ran away from home to hide out at the house in Lido Azzurro, where she was born. Her father arrived there a couple of hours later. "I'm still a virgin, if that's what you want to know," she said. He slapped her; she didn't cry. "If you do that once more, you will never, ever see me again" said Eleonora.

Luigi left.

As she was almost eighteen, it was time for Eleonora to make some decisions about her life. She was clear about her vocation; she wanted to make clothes, not study for the degrees in law or literature that her schoolmates dreamed of. She was also tired of the constant battles at home. It was a war that allowed her father to feel that he was in control of other people's lives, but she would no longer accept it. She was angry at her mother for allowing the endless pain to continue, having become part of it through her lack of rebellion against that despotic, blinkered husband who could only see his own ideas, and for allowing her children to grow in that environment. Eleonora had tried several times to convince her mother to change her life, to rebel against it, but Letizia would always answer, "Where would I go, with no money and a sick child? Who would help me look after your brother during one of his attacks?"

Eleonora spent a couple of months at the house in Lido Azzurro, contemplating her next steps. She wanted to go as far away as possible from her home, so she researched the best fashion schools in New York and decided on the New York Academy of Art. She told her mother that she was coming to lunch to inform them of her plans.

Alex was waiting for her at the gate, his arms open, shouting "Mimi!" as soon as he saw her. It was still warm that September, so her mother set the table in the garden and placed wildflowers in a vase at the center. Eleonora was greeting her mother and grandmother when her father arrived. Although she could tell he was emotional at seeing her there, he greeted her as if the moment was of no importance and soon criticized his wife for not having the meal ready. Letizia answered, "I wanted to set the table outside and I got late. It will just be a minute." Before she had finished speaking, Luigi launched himself at the table, throwing the wildflowers, plates, and glasses to the ground and sweeping off the tablecloth. Alessandro began to rock himself in his usual reaction to unease, shouting "No, uncle Gigi, go 'way. Pizzaurant, 'luminations, games, disco, spinning balls, Christmas balls, lights, steet stalls, Easter. Go 'way!" Alex suddenly grabbed an iron garden chair and threw it through the air. As it fell, it hit his grandmother on the legs. Maddalena fell to the ground, unconscious from pain. She looked dead. Eleonora screamed. Unable to stop himself, Alessandro threw himself at Letizia, punching her. Eleonora tried to stop him, but Alex had grown stronger than her. Her father called an ambulance.

That night, Luigi stayed at his mother's bedside in the hospital; she couldn't have surgery because of her age. Maddalena's thighbone was broken, and she would never be able walk again like she did before. At home, Eleonora told her mother about her decision. Letizia encouraged her. "I don't want you to witness these things ever again. You, at least, can get out." Eleonora hugged her mother, saying, "Give it up and come with me—you and Alex."

However, Letizia couldn't leave her home, the land of her origins, and the man who, despite everything, she still loved.

THE WHEELCHAIR

Eleonora waited for her grandmother, who came home in a wheelchair pushed by her son. Once there, Maddalena went straight to Alex to tell him, "Hug me, darling child. I know it wasn't you; it's a devil that gets into you. I would give my life if I could cure you, sweetheart. It's all over now, it will be okay." Alessandro was crying—he who had never before cried from emotion.

Eleonora told her father about her departure. He too would benefit from knowing she would be far away from their bubble where she had no role in the dance of Luigi, Letizia, and Alex. "How much do you need?" Luigi asked.

"I'll let you know as soon as I get to America," she answered.

"Good," answered Luigi. "Now, be careful. Don't use the telephone unless you need something."

"Goodbye, Papa. Thank you."

Eleonora left two days later. She found banknotes in her pocket—Luigi's way of saying that he loved her.

On the flight toward her new life, she read and reread the letter that Giacomo had given her before her departure. "I will never leave you. I will always be with you. I will join you as soon as I can. This is the right thing for you. Run away! Go far away! Follow your dream; this city is too small for you. Don't come back here, my love."

Eleonora imagined her mother finding solace in her room with the ochre-colored walls, her father in his white coat saying a warm goodbye to a couple carrying their child, her grandmother in her chair enjoying the last rays of sunlight in the garden surrounded by the balls of wool for her knitting and, on the tennis court, Luigino trying to teach Alessandro how to hit the ball.

NEW YORK CITY

Eleonora would never forget her first impression of New York—so imposing, full of lights and colors. Different faces and bone structures, a myriad of features, and a frenetic rhythm that she had never before contemplated, which made her ponder, *How can it be that people walk by your side without looking at you?* It wasn't like this in Sicily. She stared at everything and everyone, wondering at the various nationalities, the strange clothing, and the language that barely resembled the English she had studied at school.

She began her courses at the academy. It wasn't easy to settle in with her new classmates, so she studied some strategies to encourage friendship. Slowly, Eleonora began to dress and eat and talk like them. Her favorite destinations in Manhattan were the elegant clothing shops. Despite the proliferation of items "made in Italy," they were a world removed from the best shops in Milan and even further from those in Agrigento.

She kept up an affectionate friendship with Giacomo,

although distance had dampened their ardor. A year later he married Elena, a classmate from high school, a good girl he had known for several years.

Eleonora soon found a rhythm that worked with the energy of the Big Apple—a rented room in an apartment with other girls who were Mexican and Canadian students, the first satisfying results from her courses, and a new way of being, smiling, and behaving that was in keeping with the world of her new life! She was attentive to every tiny detail. Her hair was always fashionably straightened, her hands and nails immaculate, her clothing carefully chosen. After all, her future profession was all about appearance; how could she not start with taking care of hers?

"EPIDEMICS ARE NEVER GENETIC"

At the same time, Eleonora began to investigate autism. She made contact with an association where she met other sisters and brothers, other mothers and fathers, men and women who wanted to know more about the disorder and themselves. During the meetings, they would exchange opinions on the best approach for autistic children, how to provide them with their own life and, very importantly, how to make sure that parents could handle the daily tasks in the best way.

She contacted the Autism Research Institute, a nonprofit organization founded by Dr. Bernard Rimland, whose profound belief was "Autism is treatable." Her heart filled with hope. She discovered the Defeat Autism Now! approach, encouraged by Rimbland and the institute. It is a complex strategy combining medical and nutritional intervention in which parents and doctors worked together to treat children with autistic spectrum disorders (ASD), struggled side by side to discover the causes, improve proven treatment programs, and to celebrate and revel in the complete recovery of several of these children.

She admired the courage of the many parents of ASD children who stood up to give their accounts and interviews on television or radio to make sure they wouldn't remain isolated, fathers and mothers who would themselves become researchers and promoters of treatments, who were fighting in the front line for their children's recovery and to inform public opinion of the possible causes of this spreading disorder. Eleonora discovered that the studies researched decades earlier by her father that considered autism an emotional malady had been completely eclipsed and totally discarded. As early as 1964, Dr. Rimland, a psychologist and father of an autistic son, had discredited the Refrigerator Mother hypothesis, deeming it ridiculous and offensive to parents already struggling with the heavy toll of this terrible affliction. He had also begun to uncover the first clues that connected ASD to a biological, non-psychological disorder.

Eleonora couldn't understand why her father had never moved on from his first research but had remained petrified in that first judgment which had been superseded so long ago, or why he had always been so contrary to encouraging Alex's development. She couldn't find a satisfactory answer. Eleonora tried to take part in all the conferences that she heard about. She sought out medical magazines and scientific publications about the biological basis for ASD, in which she found out that ASD had affected only 1 in 2,000 children until the 1980s, a percentage that had multiplied incredibly over the next two decades to reach 1 in 150 by the year 2000. The most alarming data came from statistics issued by the Centers for Disease Control and Prevention (CDC), the most important government healthcare body in the United States, which, in 2008, found that 1 in 100 children were affected by ASD. In 2013, the statistic is 1 in 80.

She read that autism was called a "silent epidemic" by some researchers because it was not discussed proportionally to its increasing spread. It indeed appeared to be manifesting on the scale of an epidemic—one with largely indefinable causes despite the enormous amount of research and scientific expertise being utilized in the United States to search for information that could prove useful in putting the puzzle together. That is what autism is; a complicated puzzle.

Eleonora learned that the onset of the disorder could be connected to a combination of causes acting together involving the immune and gastrointestinal systems, and the complex metabolic and hormonal balance of the immature, still-developing body of a child. The scientists technically called it a multifactor, multiorgan, systemic disorder, meaning one that involved and disturbed the entire organism, creating permanent alterations in the intellectual, communicative, and social evolution of each of these children. At a conference in Boston, she heard it confirmed with authority that ASD should no longer be considered an emotional disorder but a biological disability, and that there should be a search for the signs of the organic damage that had affected the body first, and then the brain. Treatment would then begin with the identification and treatment of clinical symptoms in the body, not by targeting the neurological system with psychotropic drugs, which had been considered standard practice.

She also discovered that genetic studies had not produced reasons for the dizzying increase in ASD cases; genetic connections were identified in only ten percent of cases. It was, therefore, more correct to talk about a genetic vulnerability or fragility in these children in whom the coincidental presence of external and environmental factors could spark the disorder. She marveled on learning that heavy metals were indicated as one of the principal environmental factors contributing to the onset of ASD—industrial atmospheric pollution, lead particles from decades of vehicle exhaust, mercury poisoning from affected fish or from dental fillings in pregnant mothers and, no less importantly, ethylmercury contained in various vaccines. The hypothesis that emerged from these studies was that many children affected by autism were exposed to the same quantity of heavy metals as their peers, but were physiologically unable to expel the poison because of their genetic and metabolic fragility. Thus the metals tended to accumulate progressively in the body, with consequent organ damage. Eleonora was shocked to read in *The Lancet*, a prestigious British medical journal, that exposure to the lead in motorcar exhaust from the 1960s to the 1980s had drastically reduced the IQ in children already born, as well as those of future generations.

Eleonora attended a conference held by Dr. Richard Deth, who stated, "The language for defining autism is very complex; it is made up of molecules, biochemistry and neurological aspects." Dr. Deth discussed his research into environmental causes—the pesticides and heavy metals like mercury and lead that could be determining factors in these disorders. His work had made it increasingly clear to Eleonora that the latent genetic factors would manifest only if stimulated from the outside. Dr. Deth described in detail how the accumulation of metals could unleash a series of allergies and induce a state of chronic oxidative stress, ie, the accumulation of substances that attacked the cellular structures, particularly the nervous system, oxidizing them and compromising their correct functioning.

It was on this occasion that Eleonora heard about chelation therapy as essential in neutralizing the poisonous effects of metals on the organism. She learned that a chelating agent is a drug in which ligands lie around the central atom like the claws of a lobster, anchoring the metals in the tissues and encouraging their release from the system through urine and feces. However, she found it hard to accept that the foods of her homeland she loved most—bread, pasta, cheese, and milk—contain gluten and casein proteins that could be highly inflammatory and cause autoimmune brain disorders and chronic intestinal inflammation in these patients.

The outcome of this long and exhausting path of studies, interviews, and conferences for Eleonora was the revelatory understanding that some external factor afflicted these children. They were suffering not as the result of a genetic sentence, but from a disorder whose causes would, sooner or later, be clearly identified just as they had been for illnesses from the common cold to more complex inflammatory diseases, and a comprehensible reason for its exponential, epidemic diffusion would be revealed.

She was increasingly convinced that there was still a chance for Alex, who could be treated with biomedical therapies, such as a hyperbaric chamber to reduce inflammation, or chelation therapy to cleanse the organism of heavy metals. She was particularly enthusiastic about the idea that adopting an appropriate diet—one free of gluten and casein—would produce immediate results for Alex, such as reducing his habitual attacks, or mess. She was stunned to read that aggression in autistic children could simply be a result of the pain and physical unease caused by intestinal inflammation or gastroesophageal reflux. Consequently, she imagined that Alex's aggression was based on his suffering these same gastrointestinal disorders, the physical unease of a life which couldn't be expressed in words, and so exploded in a mess. It comforted her to think that a simple diet could alleviate that pain.

Eleonora devoured research papers that discussed the numerous strategies of personalized treatment for each individual child. She read about digestive enzymes for lack of food absorption or food intolerances; the importance of glutathione to encourage detoxification; the role of numerous vitamins, like B12, in strengthening the cycle of methylation and contrasting oxidative stress. She spent sleepless nights poring over scientific research papers and scrolling through miles of web pages which recorded the first-hand experiences and treatments of American families. Barraged with a wealth of information, she needed time to digest it before she could convince her parents to try something—to at least try.

"UCK, PRICK, SHIT, DICK, BALLS!"[12]

Eleonora's rented room was a miniature atelier with clothing sketches pinned all over the wall. One day, a courier knocked on the door of her apartment. She was handed a card with a map of Manhattan; an address was circled in red, as if marking a destination point. She changed to go out and, curious, went to look for that place in the midst of the crowds of people. She crossed one road, then another, checked the map, and continued on until she reached the address indicated, which was an elegant building. Standing outside the door was a man in his forties wearing a suit and tie. He handed her a bunch of keys and explained, "No need to worry; I was sent to give you these. Top floor."

The elevator took Eleonora to the top floor, where she turned the key in the lock. The door opened onto a perfectly furnished attic. In the background, the ferment of the city

---

[12] "'Fuck, prick, shit, dick, balls!"

could be seen through walls of glass. Her enchanted eyes spotted a framed photograph of her family, taken that day in Venice, which used to be on the piano in the villa. There was a letter placed next to the frame that read, "With my best wishes. I hope you like it. Be happy. I love you. Papa." She was transfixed by the photograph and the sight of Alessandro, smiling, his arms stretched into the sky. She missed her brother acutely, missed singing and playing drums with him.

She called home immediately, thanking them with all her heart—first her father, then her mother, then her grandmother. She knew that they were all crying. Eleonora, looking out onto the roofs of New York, was crying too, careful not to be overheard. When it was Alex's turn, the tears were broken with his "Fuck, prick, shit, dick, balls!" This was one of the games he always played with his sister. He would list all the swear words he knew and, for some strange reason, he could say them pretty well. Eleonora heard Luigi's voice in the background saying, "Dirty-minded boy. Does one say these bad words?" Alex replied, "Yes, yes, come here Mimi." "My dearest heart, I miss you too" said Eleonora. "Remember that you are my hero." "Okay, hero me," replied her brother.

Eleonora began to communicate with Letizia by email. She told her about her New York life and also about the treatments and diets that Alex could follow. Letizia didn't tell her that the lack of success on that front was due to her husband's obstinacy. One day at the table, Alex reached for some bread and Letizia removed the basket. Luigi asked why. "He's putting on weight," she answered. "He doesn't move enough."

Luigi raised his voice, yelling, "Give him the bread, give him food."

Letizia hesitated. "The bread we eat is bad for him, just like the pasta, cheese, and milk. He shouldn't eat gluten or casein; they are bad for him."

"Who tells you all this stuff? That scientist of a daughter? I thought she was designing costumes? I'm the doctor here. I will decide what our son eats!" He handed some bread to Alessandro and ordered him to eat it.

Letizia didn't give in. "We have to open our eyes for Alex's good. We have kept them closed for too long," she responded, and took the bread from Alex's mouth. Luigi grabbed her arm and, with his other hand, squeezed her neck hard. Alessandro upset the tablecloth, crying, "No, Uncle Gigi, go 'way, leave. Pizzaurant, 'luminations, games, Christmas, lights, drums, steet stalls, discos."

The rest was not hard to imagine.

THE FASHION PHOTOGRAPHER

Eleonora gave a party to celebrate her new apartment, to which she invited her classmates from the academy. Several boys she didn't know also came to the housewarming. Between one dance and another, she met Bob, who was handsome enough to be a model. She liked his cheeky looks. He had Irish roots, but had always lived in New York. When he was a babe in arms, his engineer father had accepted a new job across the ocean. Eleonora liked how he danced. She had never seen him at school because he was a fashion photographer, working for the best international magazines and often traveling the world for work.

At the end of the party, after the toasting and the dancing, the guests began to leave. Eleonora and Bob, now quite tipsy, were left alone. They continued to dance to the softly playing jazz, the penetrating lights from the huge windows giving the room a sensual and warm atmosphere that only that city could offer.

They had the same curls framing their faces; Eleonora straightened hers, while his were a lion's mane. She could feel the smell of her breath mingling with Bob's. Soon kisses were not enough ; they needed to go deeply into each other , to reach a point no one had ever reached before — to breathe each other. They made love all night, completely and totally, in that way unique to the madness of being twenty . Their bodies seemed sculpted under the slanting lights , their movements as smooth as if they had always been together.

They didn't waste time. The next day Bob had moved into Eleonora's apartment. He said, "I don't want to miss an instant of you. You are the most beautiful thing in creation." They were flying with happiness. They talked, they played, they cooked, they made love. Only nine days later, he had her name tattooed on his arm, the bloodied protective gauze taking the shape of a heart. They were forced to be apart for several hours a day so Eleonora could go to her courses and Bob to his shoots, but they ardently longed for evening, when they could be together again. It gave them great pleasure to meet in their apartment.

Eleonora fell in love with Bob. She loved the way he occupied space, the way he walked, and the modernity of his thoughts, and inevitably compared him to the boys from her country. He was in touch with his world; he was confident and knew he was attractive. Their life soon became a spinning wheel of fun, fashion parties, and trips to every corner of the world for fashion shoots or international *défilé*. They knew the latest news of the fashion industry, and everything about what was "in" or "out."

Eleonora let Bob advise her on her fashion collections— on her choice of fabrics, colors, and cut for the mini-collections that she needed to prepare for her academy exams. Bob appreciated her work and the meticulous preparation she put into her creations. He loved the mysterious allure she conferred to each model, drenching them in Italian flavor, a combination of antique and modern styles—the raw fabrics studded with gems, the classic fans combined with modern stylized models, and Sicilian women's shawls combined with pants cut like a man's.

The loft where they lived was strictly black and white, even the few pieces of furniture that decorated it. It was a perfect location for Bob's shoots, and soon became a permanent set with big white panels that were moved from one side to the other in the large room. "I love your generosity," Bob told her. So they passed their days happily amid lights and white sheets, models of both sexes, makeup artists, and hairdressers.

Eleonora became pregnant, and questions flooded her mind. She had her academy courses to finish and lived a world that moved too fast for a newborn's rhythms, but most of all she worried whether the child would be healthy. She felt that she was still too much a child and was not ready to become a mother. The word "mother" made her think of sacrifice, renunciation, and hatred concealed under makeup.

It was not an easy choice for Eleonora. Was she giving up her baby because she didn't want to end up like her mother, or because she was afraid that she would produce a sick child? Bob let her make her own decision, assuring her that he would support her either way. She gave up the idea of a child, and Bob didn't waver. But not a day went by that Eleonora didn't think about how he would have been. She would have called him Luca, the name of her first love.

The mutual decision for her to have an abortion was an alarm bell in a shaky relationship. They never talked about the pregnancy again. That life cut short, which should have crowned their love, had shaken her unconscious and her conscience, consequently intimating, on an invisible level, the failure of the couple as father and mother.

They split up a few months later. Bob had fallen in love with a seventeen-year-old black girl; Eleonora, at twenty-four, was already too old for him. She suffered immensely and threw herself into her work. The frenetic city life she loved so much gradually helped her to not think about Bob. Men invited her to dinner. She knew she was attractive, and she allowed herself to be courted.

"MIMI TALES"

A couple of months after her split with Bob, Eleonora graduated in fashion design. Doors previously closed were now open to her. She soon registered her label, calling it "Mimi Tales," and set up a little atelier. Her first employees were Isabella and Doris, two sisters of Sicilian heritage in their fifties. They had expert knowledge of tailoring and, until then, had worked from their homes in Brooklyn. The time had now come for them to work for a real showroom. They spoke a dialect that was almost incomprehensible to Eleonora. Having arrived in the states as babies, they had learned a kind of Sicilian-Italian language from their parents, but their vocabulary had not been affected by the linguistic evolution of the past half-century.

Eleonora could never thank them enough. Their expert embroidery, their ability to cut and to bestow a sense of times gone by to her clothes, were essential to the personality of the Mimi Tales' collections. Claire, whom she knew from the academy, managed Mimi Tales' public relations and contacts with suppliers. She soon became Eleonora's best friend and confidante, loving her work exactly as much as Eleonora did hers. They spent hours together, agreeing on every detail of the collection. The creativity was Eleonora's responsibility, while Claire simply offered her point of view. However, for anything to do with business and selling, Claire was unbeatable. She knew how to market the product well.

Eleonora spent part of her time in the showroom , sketching , while searching for *le fil rouge* that would characterize each piece in the collection . She would sometimes return home in the evening , dissatis fied by the work she had done, only to jerk awake in the middle of the night as fabulous inspiration came to her in sleep—flashes of items similar to the cape robes that Aunt Carmelina wore reimagined in modern fabric,
or her Grandmother Alba's tweed skirts and Letizia's hats and pins. Ethereal figures draped in white organza, inspired by the myth of Persephone, were characteristic of the evening dress collection.

THIMEROSAL

She continued to keep up with the world of ASD research, attending international conferences and reading articles in the *New York Times* and other American newspapers. She looked into the hypothesis that linked ASD to vaccines administered to babies between three and twenty-four months. Many American parents had noticed their children losing vitality and reducing interaction with the world around them after a vaccination, or demonstrating such bizarre behavior as running around aimlessly, staring into the distance for hours, screaming endlessly, or repeatedly flapping their arms.

The vaccinations in question contained thimerosal, a pharmaceutical compound in use since the 1930s, which has a high ethylmercury content. It is used as a preservative and an antiseptic agent. Eli Lilly and Company, then one of the world's major pharmaceutical manufacturers, developed and patented it in the 1920s. Thimerosal had been deemed safe for many years, and was approved by the United States Food and Drug Administration (FDA) for use as a preservative.

The first cases of autism were recognized in the early 1940s. Eleonora read that organic compounds represented the most dangerous form of mercury, which followed plutonium as the most poisonous substance in the world. She found out that mercury was a neurotoxin, which could cause brain damage, mental slowness, and immune dysfunction, and that it was particularly dangerous for fetuses and newborns whose organs were still developing. She also read that mercury was considered so toxic that the small amount contained in a thermometer, if released, could require the evacuation of an entire building.

The presence of mercury in vaccines was little known to the public, but research in the United States found that the amount of this element, used as a preservative in vaccines, far exceeded safe limits. An increase in cases of autism linked to the assumption of mercury into the body was also found. It was decided that the production of such vaccines would be banned; however, the vaccines still in stock would be sold. After these alarming reports were presented to the judiciary, some of which were exposed by citizens and associations, investigations were initiated to ascertain criminal liability.

Diphtheria and tetanus vaccines for infants contained about 25 micrograms (mcg) of mercury, and the pediatric hepatitis B vaccine contained 12.5 mcg. Thus, 37.5 mcg of mercury was administered together—a dose seventy times higher than the safest level recommended by the World Health Organization, which is 0.5 mcg. In the leaflets packaged with the vaccines, mercury was hidden under the names thimerosal, ethylmercury, mercuriotiolato, and sodiomertiolato.[13]

A 1998 study by British doctors at the Royal Free Hospital in Hampstead, north London, showed that the vaccination for measles, mumps, and rubella (MMR) could trigger autism due to a connection between the vaccine and inflammation of the intestine. This research showed that of twelve children who had previously been normal, each had developed an intestinal disease and nine had developed autism. According to the doctors involved in the study, eight of the children developed changes in health and behavior within six days of vaccination. In a study of another group of children, forty-six of forty-eight suffered from intestinal and behavioral problems within six days of vaccination.[14]

Numerous American families were convinced that thimerosal was the cause of ASD; the mercury level in the diphtheria, tetanus, and pertussis (DTaP) vaccine was higher than recommended federal levels, and this was believed to be the cause of unusual behaviors exhibited by children. In 2004, thimerosal was removed from many

---

[13] Libero, March 16, 2001; Corriere della Sera, June 18, 2001.

[14] Herald Sun, Melbourne, February 28, 1998; Weekly Telegraph, London March 4–10, 1998.

vaccines, but not all.[15] At the same time, epidemiological studies carried out by scientists with links to pharmaceutical companies were trying to discredit the correlation between vaccines and ASD, although they were never able to fully refute the existence of cause and effect. Immersed in her reading, Eleonora wondered, *Did my father give Alex the recommended vaccinations as a child?*

Luigi had followed the orthodox medical recommendations of the time to prevent illness in his son, who was still in diapers. And so Alessandro had been subjected to the recommended vaccinations—measles, mumps, rubella, and varicella.

As Eleonora looked for other sources that linked ASD and mercury, she came across the issue of mercury amalgam dental fillings. The WHO had recognized that dental amalgam was one of the greatest sources of exposure to mercury not only in adults, but also in newborns, because the metal was easily transferred to the fetus through the placenta or by breastfeeding. Mercury vapor, continuously released from amalgam dental fillings, causes mercury poisoning.

---

[15] Heated debate about mercury-containing vaccines continues in the United States on both the scientific and political fronts. Only 20% of the cases against the U.S. government for damages caused by vaccinations have been successful; the others have been rebutted for lack of evidence.

There was a substantial rise in dental care during the 1990s, and mercury amalgam was the material most used for fillings. As neither vaccinations nor dental care were provided free, mostly upper-middle socioeconomic groups took advantage of both. This historical context was in line with a popular thesis that ASD was most common among wealthier social groups. *Did my mother go to the dentist when she was pregnant with Alessandro?* Eleonora pondered. Of course she had.

Eleonora thought she might never find a comprehensive explanation for the cause of her brother's disorder, and realized that she was more interested in researching solutions that would relieve the consequences of it in his daily life—reducing the suffering from his continual gastrointestinal problems and the chronic viral infections which were getting worse with every passing year. *What can I do for him?* she asked herself.

Her frustration increased along with her anger at her father, who refused to consider any sort of treatment or hope. She had tried various times to convince him to move to New York with the family so that Alex could be properly looked after, but Luigi's answer was always the same. "You look after your family and I will look after mine. There is no hope for your brother, do you understand? He just needs your mother at his side all the time." Eleonora was always stunned at being unable to find any level of dialogue with her father, and he ended the conversation there.

She was aware that her father demonstrated his love for her through his generosity. Thanks to his moral and financial support, she had been able to follow her dream and leave her hometown to discover the wider world. How could he allow Alex's life to pass by without at least attempting to find treatment? It was something Eleonora truly could not understand. She was unable to find sufficient motive for her father, so generous with one child, yet quite the opposite with the other. Treatment for Alex would also mean treating Letizia, Luigi, and Eleonora for the constant pain that afflicted them as well. Furthermore, did her father not consider the fact that Alex was going to be an inheritance he would leave for Eleonora to look after? She told herself, *There must be a natural right to good health and a normal, or at least better, life. Why should Alex still be treated with psychotropic drugs instead of a measured medical approach and behavior therapy?*

THE TWO BOILERS

Her extensive research had shown Eleonora that most ASD children were afflicted with gastrointestinal problems like her brother, especially those with regressive autism, in which the natural development of the first years of life was not only interrupted but reversed, with the sufferer losing abilities he had previously acquired.

Eleonora attended a DAN conference that focused on the links between intestinal inflammation and cerebral inflammation. She paid particular attention to Dr. Nicola Antonucci, a DAN practitioner, who stated, "There are essentially two 'boilers' to consider: the intestinal boiler and the cerebral boiler. The intestinal boiler is certainly the principal producer of inflamed cytokines, the inflammatory messengers that enter the system and activate specific inflammatory cells in the brain. Inflammation is stimulated in the microglial cells, but it is a secondary process in that it does not take place in that organ but has been stimulated by the intestine. This is why treating the intestine produces an enormous improvement on the second 'boiler,' the brain, and why treating the intestine effectively means treating the stereotypes: hyperactivity, difficulties with language and communication, the attention and learning deficit, sleep disorders, obsession, and tendency to impulsive and aggressive behavior. Intestinal inflammation is exacerbated by the assumption of gluten and casein in foods. These proteins alter the permeability of the intestinal walls, allowing toxic substances and bacteria to pass through, which stimulate the immune system into producing inflammatory mediators that travel to the brain, compromising its functioning, and then transform into opiate compounds which foster addiction."

It was not a coincidence that children with ASD were always desperate for bread, milk, and related products. *Why not treat Alex's intestine instead of treating him as mentally ill?* Eleonora thought. *Who knows how many times he must have suffered senseless gastrointestinal pain? What if his daily meds, which are supposed to heal his psyche, are making his gastrointestinal apparatus even more sensitive?*

She watched hopefully as several American researchers began to insist on an interdisciplinary scientific approach combining neuropsychiatry, gastroenterology, immunology, and nutrition. Sectors that were generally considered to have opposite approaches in both diagnosis and therapy needed to connect to find complete solutions. Eleonora wanted to do something for her brother and fast, before he became an adult. The specialists that she had questioned had been very clear; the longer the delay in treatment, the less likely the possibility of recovery.

She was devastated by a sense of impotence. She felt a growing sense of guilt about being able to have everything life had to offer, while her brother couldn't. He couldn't be free, he couldn't say "I love you," he couldn't find a girl. Should she give in to her father's stubbornness and let Alex's life go by without making any effort or hope for a change of heart from her father?

Letizia's phone call temporarily distracted her from this struggle.

THE END OF AN ERA

Letizia tearfully informed Eleonora of the death of her mother, Alba. Eleonora's grandmother had passed in the silence of her solitude, as discreetly as she had lived. Alba had always given her love unconditionally, had never been a burden on anyone, and she prepared to greet death in the same way, waiting serenely in bed. Since the death of her husband Giovanni five years before, the isolation of the farmhouse had become too much for her. Her heart was full of the pain caused by the absence of her favorite child, Letizia, who had been categorically forbidden to visit by Luigi. Her daughter felt guilty for not having spent more time with her.

Seated on the sofa, Eleonora listened to her mother in silence, speechless. She had always been very fond of her grandmother, who had passed on her love for literature, philosophy, and art. "Don't worry about material goods; feed your mind with poetry and love," she would say. On the bedside table, her children, Ferdinando, Letizia, and Laura, had found poetry written in a old style hand which evoked

times gone by.
Don't ask me what I need,
but who I need.

It is you who nourish me.

You are my heaven, my son, and I your sea.
When the sun smiles in the blue,
the sea lets everything become sparkling;
and when among clouds, the sky grieves with tears
of rain, the heartbroken sea collects all those tears
on himself.[16]

Letizia tried to keep her grief under control while speaking to Eleonora on the phone. She did not want to show her sadness to Alex, but he continued to repeat, "Where is Granma? Ah, in the sky with Gandpa! Dammit!"

That day, Letizia's guilt at not having spent more time with her mother to obey her husband's wishes exploded in anger at Luigi. She felt suspended in the air, in a kind of limbo, conscious of the life she was living and yet resigned. She couldn't find a reaction.

---

[16] See Alba's poem written in her own hand on page XVII.

Letizia was not able to do what was needed to be able to rebel against something so strongly rooted—to find inner silence, summon the strength to gather herself in her pain and listen to her own point of view, her true need to make herself respected as wife and mother.

There were times she considered leaving her husband and fleeing with her son, but after a night's sleep, the idea dissolved the next day. It was as if she thought something could change without her making changes herself.

For Letizia, every day had become like the one before. Hours punctuated by breakfast; morning cleaning while Alex was playing drums; lunch; Alex's afternoon rest, because if she didn't rest with him, he would not sleep; television; dinner; and then to bed as quickly as possible so the silence of those dinners weighed on her as little as possible. At times, the silence was broken by Alex's sudden attacks.

He too could not bear the repetition of the days, with everything exactly as it had been the day before, and the lacerating heaviness that his parents created. This added to his physical suffering.

For a boy who loved parties and festivities and joy, that silence was unbearable. "Wouldn't it be easier to take a weight off these souls by laughing, playing the piano, dancing?" Alex seemed to say. "What is the point of rancor and resentment?" That was the essence of life for Alessandro—laughter, dance, and enjoyment.

One day, Letizia noticed Luigi placing something in the earth of the main flowerbed in the garden, between a pine tree and a hibiscus. She went over and found a rhomboid-shaped stone, similar to that of a gravestone, made of calcarenite,[17] the same porous ochre stone as the Doric temples. She bent over it curiously. There was a phrase from Genesis engraved upon it; "We are dust and to dust we will return." She was speechless. Husband and wife were no longer communicating; time had stopped in that house. Everything was static, identical, unchanging. Luigi had extinguished every form of enthusiasm for life. In his heart, he believed that only death would heal their suffering.

Given this atmosphere of tension, Alex's attacks became increasingly frequent but, of course, Luigi and Letizia did not tell their daughter.

---

[17] Calcarenite is a type of clastic sedimentary rock, formed by calcareous particles the size of sand. It is often of biological origin—from fossils of marine organisms, and/or fragments of shells of shellfish, algae, or foraminifera. It is porous, which allows rainwater and the waters returned by the underlying clay to exude a compound rich in fossils, with a color ranging from reddish yellow to light yellow.

THE LAWYER

She met Philip playing golf. Italian-American and New York–born, he had an athlete's physique and an intellectual's glasses. He began to avidly court her, inviting her to dinner, to skiing weekends in Vancouver, to play golf and tennis. He soon declared his love and his desire to be with her all his life. "If you were to leave me, I would kill myself," he would say. Eleonora was enchanted by his words, the splendid invitations, and the red roses unfailingly delivered every other day. It wasn't long before they started living together; Phil left his rented apartment and went to live in Eleonora's loft. He was a lawyer, and the fact that he was very practical, with a profession so different from the often frivolous world of fashion, made Eleonora feel protected and safe. They enjoyed themselves together enormously; the same age, they shared a love of sport and travel. But they would end up in front of the TV, watching their favorite shows, eating hamburgers and fries with ketchup in bed. His intellectual's glasses hid a love of cannabis. Eleonora was not shocked when she found out, but she was surprised.

Several months of cohabitation later, Phil no longer appeared to be investing in their relationship as he had done at the start. He had happily slipped into a daily routine without worrying about keeping their relationship alive. In the name of the love in which she strongly believed, Eleonora had turned a blind eye to his negative traits, such as his meanness. His sweetness and total adoration of her had won her over. Phil ardently desired to have a child with her. Every time he mentioned this, she would reply, "I can't wait to hold a baby Phil in my arms, but first I must do all the tests I can to make sure we have healthy children."

Eleonora gathered her courage and began to address the question of having children with the doctors she had met. The tests she could have done in the United States were aligned with the most recent research. She had her hair analyzed and her urine tested for porphyrin to assess the levels of toxic, heavy metals like mercury. The doctors she was in contact with explained that accumulations of mercury, lead, and aluminum in the body from alimentary and environmental pollution were generally expelled via the feces and sebum. However, a low level of metal in the hair would indicate that these elements were being retained and were poisoning vital organs, putting a fetus at risk of ASD. While waiting for the outcome of the tests, she was advised to follow a diet and take supplements that would detoxify her system from a potential overload of metals.

Eleonora was focused on work and her ASD research, but she was realizing that the couple was arguing much more frequently—generally about the financial management of their family unit. He never did the grocery shopping; "It's a woman's job," he would say. He objected to paying someone to clean, declaring, "My mother always did the cleaning; I don't understand why you don't want to." Eleonora soon began to chafe at this approach, which reminded her of the hometown she had fled. The arguments continued, spilling over into who was to pay the building fees, the utility bills, and even for dinners out. However, when they made peace, Phil, who knew how to get his girlfriend to forgive him, would say, "You are my other half; I will never leave you. I promise to change. I want a child with you."

"We will start trying seriously once the autumn/winter shows are done," Eleonora answered. "I promise."

THE PHONE CALL IN THE NIGHT

That year, Eleonora and Phil spent the New Year's holiday in Rio de Janeiro. The joyful approach of the Brazilian people created a magical atmosphere. There were continuous parties on Copacabana beach and the environment was joyful and entertaining. During one of these parties, in the midst of the crowd, Eleonora began to feel sick her legs trembling, she felt as if she about to faint and lost control. It was a panic attack. She had never had one before. She thought she was going to die that very instant; she couldn't breathe, and she felt the ground disappear from under her feet. Phil picked her up, pushed his way through the crowd, stopped a taxi, and took her back to the hotel. He laid her on the bed where she woke up, still pale. The sounds of the party filtered in from that beautiful beach they could see from their room. "Rest now," said Phil "I am going to look for a doctor." He kissed her sweaty forehead and left the room.

Eleonora fell into a deep sleep, which was broken by

the ringing of her cell phone. She answered to hear a sobbing Letizia tell her, "Your father tried to kill me. I have a black eye. Alessandro defended me. It's night, everyone is asleep now. Your brother and I can't stay here any longer. I'm packing our bags and I'll hide them under the bed. As soon as your father has gone out, we will leave. We're coming to join you."

"Okay, Mamma, I'll be here for you. Be careful," she said.

Phil returned; he hadn't been able to find a doctor. Eleonora told him about the call, adding, "My love, my mother and brother will be staying with me until they find the right place to live. I think four of us will be too many in the loft. Could you stay at your parents for a short while? We could even think about renting another apartment for us. Give me the time to spend a few months with them; then I will finally be all yours and we can think about this child."

"Of course," answered Phillip. "That's the reason for your panic attack! When your parents argue, you always feel it and feel sick. Just know that I am by your side, my love. You have all my respect and admiration. I'll take care of your mother's legal affairs too, if she wants."

"Thanks Phil. I couldn't do this without your help."

Eleonora felt it essential to dedicate time to her brother and mother; she was the only member of the family who could make a difference. The time had come to attempt Alessandro's rehabilitation with the right therapies. An almost maternal love for him beat somewhere in her; she had not managed to remove that ancient sense of guilt that she carried. Running far away had not been enough to cut all the emotional ties to her life with her family; on the contrary, they had become more vivid than ever. Time and distance had not done anything on that front. Now she could finally do something—she could find an answer to all her questions and cut the umbilical cord with her biological family to start a new life with Phil. Supported by her partner, she knew that she would find the courage she needed to manage this difficult time.

They returned to New York the next day, their eyes touched with a light melancholy. The two awoke that Sunday morning in the nest that had witnessed and nourished their love. He went out to run in Central Park to reorder his thoughts and accommodate these latest changes. Eleonora stayed at home, staring at the walls, listening to the silence, to her mood, staring at every object. In a couple of days it would all change; new people would be living there—Letizia, Alex, and herself.

Eleonora sat on the white corner sofa facing the glass walls, the same sofa that had seen her and Phil sleep until the early light of dawn : make love with candlelight and jazz, watch their favorite TV show, seen them angry, tearful, and sometimes depressed. They both loved that house so much! What would happen the next day?

Phil was going to move in with his parents until the time came for them to be together again. Eleonora thought about her father and how he would react to the separation from his wife and son. She knew full well that he would consider this the ultimate betrayal, and that his hatred for his wife would only increase with such an offense. He would feel betrayed by Eleonora, too, and would see her as his wife's accomplice. Luigi's suffering would be endless—solitude, a mother in a wheelchair who needed looking after, and a house to start learning about. He didn't even know where the cutlery was kept or how to light the cooker. Eleonora was moved by the thought of her father in that situation, but she was also extremely angry with him. *If he hadn't been so stubborn and inflexible, stuck in his own mind-set,* she thought, *they wouldn't have reached this point—Letizia and Alex forced to flee in secret.* She didn't want to think about her father too much for the time being. The priority was treatment for Alex and a quiet, dignified life for Letizia. She needed to ensure that the step from small town to big city did not cause any additional trauma.

Eleonora would never forget that morning, which was an important moment in shaping her life. She decided to celebrate the change by buying a big Christmas tree with flashing lights and colorful decorations. Even if it was March, it would make Alex feel at home. In Alex's imagination, New York was the

Christmas city with its incredibly tall trees, famous lights, sleighs, and multiple Father Christmases handing out sweets on the street.

"MIMI, NEW YO', FUNNN, PLANE, SO MANY NICE THINGS"

Two days later, Eleonora welcomed Letizia and Alex at the airport. The international arrivals terminal was thronged with relatives and friends waiting to embrace their loved ones arriving on that flight from Italy. Eleonora pushed her way to the barrier at the front so she would spot her mother and brother's faces. The flow of people pulling their baggage moved quickly and politely forward. Some looked anxious as they searched the crowd, hoping to spot those familiar smiles as soon as possible. It was almost as if their lives, still hanging in the air in that moment, were entirely entrusted to the people coming to greet them at this airport in this new city. Eleonora was excited. She wondered how Alex had behaved on the plane.

Suddenly, a drum roll attracted everyone's attention, coming from somewhere among the crowd of passengers. The melody of "Jingle Bells" wafted through arrivals. Alex spotted Eleonora from a distance and, eyes sparkling with happiness, drummed even harder as he approached her. He started to shout, "Mimi, New Yo', funnn, plane, Christmas, lights, so many nice things." Eleonora hugged him tightly, answering in the same language. Letizia appeared, laden down with suitcases and fatigue. The two women hugged. "You'll see, everything will be fine now," said Eleonora, "You finally decided to do it; that's the most important thing."

They loaded the bags into the car and headed home. During the drive, Letizia told Eleonora that Alex had been invited by the pilot into the cabin to watch the landing procedure, and how excited he had been. He had loved seeing the city, lit up, from above. Eleonora asked Letizia about the bandage on her left ring finger. "A present from your father in the last argument."

"Okay. I don't want to know any more," Eleonora said.

Alex added, "Papa broken it, finger broken Mamma, dammit!"

"Let's turn on the radio and sing!" Eleonora exclaimed. They sang Pooh songs at the top of their voices for the rest of the journey.

That finger stayed bent forever. Letizia's hand never returned to its previous state; it became an invalid. It was almost as if Luigi had left a brand on his wife's body as a permanent memory that felt like a sentence.

When they arrived home, Eleonora opened the front door and talked to Sun, as she called her apartment. "Sun, this is Alex and this is Mamma. From today, they will be living here. It's important you treat them well."

Alex exclaimed "Lovely, Sun, Mimi! Nice Christmas tree! Tank you Mimi."

Phil joined them that evening; he had met Eleonora's family the year before during a holiday in Sicily. Alex was happy to see him again and greeted him, "Hi friend! Me go funfair, you?" Philip didn't understand Italian nor Alex's language, so he simply nodded.

After some initial chat, Letizia told them about the latest unpleasant events with her husband. She was obviously strained, sadness making her eyes dark, but she also appeared to have decided that she would no longer accept any abuse. She was in a fighting mood and asking for justice now, furious at nearly forty years spent with a man who had not treated her well. Phil started the process of separation between Letizia and Luigi.

From that night on, Eleonora slept on the sofa and Phil moved in with his parents to allow Letizia and Alex to occupy the room he had shared with Eleonora for three years.

Eleonora reorganized her days. She spent her mornings at the showroom, bringing her mother and brother with her, while the afternoons were spent on medical appointments for Alex. Her schedule, until then filled with work lunches, dance lessons, magazine interviews, and the best parties in New York, was now occupied with appointments with the best doctors and therapists in the city. It was with great happiness that Letizia and Eleonora began to dedicate themselves to Alex's recovery. A world of new hope, previously unexplored and impossible, took shape. Her love for her brother would push her beyond what she had ever thought or suspected possible.

The disorder that had characterized Alex's life was not the only issue she needed to face. On their first day in New York, Eleonora had noticed that her mother moved her head in an odd way, with a light, continuous rocking. She thought it could be Parkinson's disease or something similar. Eleonora took a deep breath and told her mother that she had noticed this.

"Let's think about Alex," Letizia replied. "I can wait; it's due to anxiety."

"Maybe," Eleonora acknowledged, "but unless we're sure that you are well, how are we going to help Alex?" Convinced, Letizia agreed to a checkup at one of the most prestigious clinics in the city.

Letizia was diagnosed with the onset of Parkinson's Disease, and so she too began a program of hospital stays and appointments with specialized teams. Professor Strozzi, the director of the clinic, a man with Italian roots, was convinced that Letizia's treatment would provide good results because her illness was detected early. "My dear lady" he said, "the anger and pain accumulated in all these years had to be expressed somewhere! You need peace, serenity, and harmony now. Didn't you say that your husband was a doctor? How come he never noticed?" Letizia didn't reply, her stunned gaze indicating the mass of thoughts tumbling through her mind.

She decided then and there that there was no room for more challenges to face, and she would not allow this new thing into her life. She informed her daughter, "I am not going to let this win. I'm not even going to let this be called by its name. It has to be gone from my life." From that day on, they did their best not to mention it, and Letizia began treatment for Parkinson's.

A month after their arrival in New York, everything had a different flavor, one that still seemed a little bitter because the situation was still hard, and the treatments to heal Alex and control Letizia's illness were invasive, albeit necessary.

Eleonora's heart screamed with rage as she looked back at the past, at every precious, wasted day that could have seen their lives lived to the full with serenity and joy. She tried to make herself think constructive thoughts. To gather her courage and reassure herself, she thought, *It's all fine.*

Nothing is lost. We'll start again now with determination and with the awareness that everything will change.

Alex made progress on his new gluten- and casein-free diet; his attacks noticeably reduced in number, and his language became more comprehensible. A constant flow of therapists monitored him regularly, using Applied Behavior Analysis (ABA). These professional educators spent many hours with Alex, encouraging him to develop fluency in language, to improve his observational and communication skills, and to keep the stereotypical, aggressive, and angry behaviors in check.

The ABA method was the latest American approach to attempt language recovery in children with ASD. Alex was no longer a child, but his mother and sister still hoped that therapy would improve his abilities, even if only a little. Sometimes Alex would ask his mother, "Uncle Gigi come here? Everyone at Mimi's?"

Letizia would comfort him. "Yes darling, Papa will come here sooner or later. He loves you very much, and he thinks about you all the time."

BEST HUSBAND IN THE WORLD, BEST FATHER IN THE WORLD

Luigi felt that he was the victim of the ultimate offense he could imagine—the dissolution of his family. He could feel hatred for his wife growing in his heart, to which he added his anger at Eleonora, whom he imagined to be his wife's accomplice. Months went by. He continued to hope that his family would return, but his pride would not allow him to change his behavior. Phil tried periodically to communicate with him, man to man, and explain that his approach was ethically wrong, but Luigi would cut him off, insisting that he was the victim and that his wife's stubbornness was to blame for everything. "I am the best husband in the world and the best father in the world!" he would repeat, excluding the possibility of broaching any kind of meaningful dialogue.

Villa Letizia was enveloped in a different atmosphere now; it looked tired, the tennis net sagged to the ground, there were weeds in the garden, and the nativity statues on the terrace had been blown over by the wind. Alex would never have allowed them to be out of place; he was always quick to line them up.

Luigi often spent time at the far end of the villa, on the cliffs, staring at the horizon. The roiling sea and the waves breaking on the cliffs interrupted the silence. He had retired, and had removed all his books, his framed diplomas, and conference awards and honors from his office at the hospital.

Every now and again, he would go for a walk in the village square with his mother in her wheelchair and her caregiver. He felt lost in the midst of people, an anonymous figure. He recognized the children that he used to attend sitting at the bar, now adults, but no one greeted him except for an elderly man who raised his hat when Luigi went by.

SPERMATOZOA

With no little effort and thanks to Isabella's and Doris's hard work, Eleonora managed to present her autumn/winter collection. The sisters were perfectly in tune with the label's needs, and well aware of the level of perfection that Mimi Tales required in every detail. They worked hard on the hand-embroidered fabrics and in finishing every piece and, aware that this was a difficult moment for Eleonora, they tried to please her as much as they could.

At the fashion show, Letizia and Alex were seated in the front row alongside the heart of New York's couture industry. Alex found the photographers massed in front of the catwalk, with their long lenses, fascinating. Letizia was proud of her daughter. She had never seen a live show, only the DVDs Eleonora had sent to her in Sicily. Phil wasn't there; he was busy at work and, in his heart of hearts, considered Eleonora's work more of a hobby than a real profession.

The show was a triumph. During the applause, Alex cried out, "Well done Mimi, lovely girls, dammit!" to which her mother replied, "Shut up, you'll get us thrown out!" Luckily, no one understood Italian, and took Alex's enthusiasm for the models as an ovation for the designer. The wealthiest women in the city fought their way backstage to book the pieces they had just seen from Isabella, Doris, and Claire. Each was unique and finished by expert hands. Enthusiastic at the show's success, Eleonora was very upset that her love had not been there to celebrate the moment with her.

The next day, Eleonora met Phil to tell him about the evening. He was shifty and looking for an excuse to argue. "I know you're busy at work and that you can't waste precious time," said Eleonora, "but when are you going to get around to renting us a flat? Don't you think about us?" Do you think it's normal to make love in your office when your colleagues have gone?"

"The truth is that I am worried about the amount of time you put into your label. What if there is not enough left for me and our family?" Phil asked.

"I love my work," she answered, "and you should be happy about my success, but you didn't even come to the show. Perhaps you would be happier with a girlfriend who works in a bank, who would placate your anxieties and keep your dinner warm."

Several weeks later, Phil made another woman pregnant. Ironically, she did indeed work for a bank. Phil's spermatozoa had not been able to wait for Eleonora. He gave no plausible reason for the breakup; he didn't have the courage. Only many months later did Eleonora learn from a mutual friend that he had had a child and, shortly afterwards, had married the girl. Eleonora never understood why Phil had continued to send her messages of love and sex during the nine months that must have marked his child's gestation. She wished she could have packed them up in a wedding present for his wife.

She suffered greatly for a while, losing over twenty pounds in three weeks. She couldn't believe that this Phil was the same person who had said to her so many times, "Without you, I'd die. I will love you for the rest of my life; I want a child with you." Her thoughts massed one on top of another, but she found nothing that soothed her pain. Whom had she spent three years of her life with? Someone she no longer recognized. She woke up retching, and it continued until she went to sleep. She felt betrayed in the most intimate and precious part of her being—her maternity, which had always been her most vulnerable and fragile point. Only the week before the show, she had picked up the test results, which gave her the all-clear. "My love, I'm holding the results in my hand. I can have healthy children. Isn't that wonderful?" she had said happily to him.

"Yes, that's great. We'll talk later; I'm at work now." The reason for certain behaviors almost always come out in time, but at the moment it occurs, one tries very hard not to see.

Eleonora just wanted to sleep all day so she wouldn't have to think, but she had to keep fighting. Happiness helped Alex; no crying, complaints, or outbursts of any type were allowed in front of him. She had to keep calm to keep her brother calm. Then, one day, she woke up and realized that she no longer had any feelings for Phil and was happy to be free of an immature boy. She could now turn a new page, trusting that, sooner or later, the love of her life would appear.

Letizia and Eleonora often agonized over Alex's future. They inspected various residential centers providing specialized care, where he could even learn a profession. After careful examination, they made requests on his behalf at a few of these places. They soon received a positive answer from one of the best—the Developmental Learning Center, a pleasant community situated on a low hill. Letizia and Eleonora were thrilled that there was finally a concrete opportunity for Alex to attend a specialized center where he would be able to paint, play his drums during music hours, exercise, and learn many things that he did not yet know. Naturally, at the center, his gluten- and casein-free diet would continue, the diet that Letizia and Eleonora now also followed in solidarity.

SHINING EYES

And so Alex began a completely new chapter in his life. He began to socialize, enjoying mimicking the sounds of the new language around him which, inexplicably, he sometimes understood better than his mother. The ASD Recovery Center approach recommended a gradual distancing from the mother figure, so Letizia was allowed to spend three hours of the morning with him while he was doing his activities, after which she was obliged to leave for the good of the patient. He didn't complain when he saw her go, but his eyes filled with tears. Letizia also cried when she turned to leave. She found it hard to separate from her son; she would stay at the center for hours, spying on Alex from the garden without his knowing.

After this part of her day, Letizia would take the subway and meet Eleonora at the showroom. There she could at least speak Sicilian with the seamstresses. However, Isabella and Doris gradually began to teach her English. For practice and to make daily progress, she would chat away happily to her daughter's clients. She had a natural talent for public relations which she had never realized, or perhaps had simply never been given the chance to express except among the guests invited to parties at the villa. Everyone found Letizia very charming, and it wasn't long before she was part of a social circle in New York high society, her diary increasingly full of bridge and poker games.

Letizia was enjoying a taste of life, as if she were a child discovering the world for the first time. She began to like the idea of an existence where fun and enjoyment were vital components. Finally free to breathe, she increasingly wondered, *How on earth did I bear that world?* Now she was free to do what she thought best without someone there ready to censure her every action.

When she first arrived in New York, she told every person she met about the difficulties she had lived through. It was her way of getting rid of everything that had accumulated inside for so many years. It was a kind of therapy she administered to herself. She would start talking in Italian, often to people who didn't understand a word she was saying, which was sometimes preferable. She frequently repeated the same scenarios—the nightmare of her husband's afternoon nap, when she would have to keep the children quiet for fear that he would wake. "When Luigi slept to recharge his batteries, to ensure his best form when playing cards, there had to be total silence. If he could hear a fly beat its wings, there was disaster. The children were not free to play because he had to sleep." Her children had learned to be as silent as cats, walking on tiptoes, able to move without disturbing the air around them, like feathers in the wind. This allowed them to detect the smallest or most distant noise. "It was as if they had radar. That villa was full of noises. The quieter it was, the more the children would enjoy competing to recognize sounds that I couldn't even hear."

They would, finally, never have to deal with that deafening silence again. Letizia adored New York because there was no chance of being in silence anywhere; the buzz and rush that characterized the city were essential to her recovery. She was recuperating from the grief over the end of her marriage and dealing well with her separation from Alex, with whom she had been joined at the hip, both part of the same person, for twenty-five years.

It was wonderful to see her in her new world. Letizia talked about her previous life as if it were of interest to the entire human race and, even if her listeners didn't understand, she launched into descriptive gesticulations. However, she was unable to find an explanation for her husband's profound sense of guilt, sacrifice, and duty. These were, for him, the only acceptable components of a proper Catholic life. Luigi would deem anything else—happiness, joy, a carefree existence— negative components suitable only for the superficial and people unworthy of respect.

"Happiness leads to licentiousness," Letizia would say, imitating Luigi's voice, "to lust, enjoyment of sensual pleasure, mortal sins!" She told people about the meals riddled with guilt. She mimicked his posture, head bent and eyes lowered to the plate, making her listeners laugh. Then she would add, in Luigi's imperious tone, "Libidinous dishes, which sate the senses, are only permitted if drenched in a sauce of guilt and unease." The head bent over the plates was a mea culpa for the joy previously experienced. And so the family meal became a sort of torture; no one dared to speak or comment on the day's events. Life outside that microcosm was not even contemplated in conversation, and any mention of it only produced those silences and that sad, tired, angry, lifeless atmosphere. The aim during a meal was to try to bring it to an end as soon as possible, and to flee into one's bedroom for an afternoon nap or for the night. This all became increasingly obvious once Eleonora had left the house.

They had all always slept a lot in that villa; to kill time, to hasten the end, to suffer less. Now, in contrast, life was beginning for Letizia. Luigi had always loved his family deeply, but in his own unusual way, different than the general understanding of love among the human race.

Letizia told her daughter one day, "Your father has always dreamed of having the perfect family. 'Perfect' meant a family made up of many persons, but moved from one mind—his mind. Luigi conceded just one point of view, and that was his own. It was the only one he could see. If someone was trying to externalize their thoughts, Luigi would have immediately stopped with his usual phrase, 'But you do not even know what you mean; you're wrong.' He did not want to evolve. And if anyone dared to act without considering his point of view, they were a goner and immediately had to pay a penalty.

"But your father has also done good. Remember Luigino? The little boy with no shoes that you hated? Thanks to your father, he has graduated in medicine and now works in London. Your father has never been able to show us his love; perhaps, secretly, he would have liked to. None of us is perfect. But I have seen him get up in the night to check that you were both sleeping well and, in secret, he would always give you a kiss. Your grandmother Maddalena always said that children should be kissed when they are asleep so that they don't get spoiled."

"Why did you stay so long?" asked Eleonora.

"Out of love. One does that out of love. Out of hope that, sooner or later, he would change. He would show me love only in silence, when we made love in those early years, and he would stare at me with shining eyes, hugging me close as if he were a child."

OF ALL KIND

Eleonora was stunned to see her mother in this previously unknown role. Full of enthusiasm for her new life and aware of having lived in a cage until now, Letizia did not intend to go back. At almost sixty years of age, she was finally going to start enjoying life. She was still a beautiful woman who cared about her appearance, although when Eleonora said, "Now you can find a man too!" she answered, "No way, absolutely out of the question. Over my dead body! Men are good for nothing." Then she would add, "I just want my children to be happy. If I am busy enjoying myself, it is only to distract me from missing your brother."

Luigi was also deeply missing Alex, but he reacted in a different way. He stared at the sea, lost in thought, on the bench in the villa garden, distracted only by the voice of Catalina, his mother's Polish caregiver, who looked after him too. "Doctor, it's ready, come and eat." He had been retired almost a year, but these days no one even invited him to play poker; there had been too many arguments with his gaming friends over money.

The town had changed, too. There were many old people and foreign faces. The new people were immigrants who flocked in droves from Lampedusa to stay awhile in the region. Villa Letizia quickly became a crossroads for floods of people of all nationalities, coming and going. Luigi had decided to take care of the penniless immigrants in need of help and medical attention without asking anything in return.

But his greatest suffering was caused by Alex's absence. Over the past months, he had become aware of how much he missed his son's enthusiasm for life and his joy at being alive. He had not properly acknowledged the value of this happiness, and now he felt that he was suffocating in that house without the sounds of drumming or swearwords pronounced in Alex's unique accent. He spoke to him on the telephone every day, saying, "Darling, I love you. You'll see, I'll come and get you from there and bring you home so we can play tennis and drums together." "Yes, Uncle Gigi, I come there," Alex answered, he who had always longed to play with his father. Alex missed his father, too.

Luigi couldn't sleep through the night; the thought of Alex in a center, surrounded by people with disorders more profound than his, made him uneasy. He was sure that the boy was unhappy. How could Alex, who loved parties and all forms of entertainment, be at ease among all kinds of sick people? The strangest thoughts fed Luigi's unease. *How can he keep going without his mother at his side, he who has always lived with his mother and in his mother? What if they've been giving him sedatives? If they've been hurting him or if someone tried to sodomize him, would he be able to defend himself?*

Luigi began to call Eleonora every day, using every weapon he could to convince her to send Alex home. "It's impossible, Papa" she would reply. "I have done so much to find him the best treatment. He is fine and being looked after by the best specialists in New York. He comes home to us on the weekends."

Luigi would reply, "He's not happy there. I've promised him to get him out. Your mother is a disgrace; she has stooped to any means to free herself of her son and live the good life. If Alex stays there, I will cut your mother off, I will take the house from her, I will prove that she is sick and not capable of having custody of her son. I swear it. I want my son back."

Eleonora felt like drowning; once again, her father was threatening her. She was still working on getting over her split with Philip, she had just moved into a new apartment and was surrounded by boxes, and her mother and brother were just beginning to lead their own lives. She wondered, *Where am I in all this?* She felt that she had lost track of herself, that there was something she had been hiding for years behind a compliant smile while she tried to keep everything together. Now, none of these methods worked, and she felt completely empty, lost, and drained of hope. She no longer believed in love, nor did she trust others. She couldn't even throw herself into that whirling social life she had lived before her family's arrival. A kind of lethargy took over.

NAMASTE

Eleonora decided that it was time for her to go traveling. Every year, Claire went to Kerala to buy precious fabrics for the summer collection. That year, she told Claire she would go herself. She had always loved India, and now was the right time for her to explore and also find some serenity. She set off with a rucksack and little fuss, again alone with herself in the same solitude that had enveloped her in her bedroom at the villa, the room with the ochre walls. She was fleeing in a search for something that would solve the questions of her life.

She arrived in Trivandrum. The city was buzzing with rickshaws and scooters, some with four people on board, mostly families with a mother, father, and children. Every vehicle on the road regularly honked its horn to warn of its imminent arrival. Eleonora was delighted by the people, who smiled endlessly with their big, black, good-natured eyes. The scent of turmeric and other spices, mingled with the stench of gaseous pollutants from the 1980s-style cars, was pervasive.

Eleonora decided to find a place to stay in the countryside

just outside Trivandrum. Despite finding the noise and bustle of the city fascinating, she didn't want to cope with it; she needed silence and calm. She took a rickshaw to the Satsangam Lodge.

Leaving behind the smells and sounds of the city, she ventured into the lush countryside filled with ancient palm trees and endless silkworm plantations. Paddies of tall green rice were dotted with the bright colors of saris worn by the women who floated across the landscape, holding baskets. Female figures, dressed in dark red, pale purple, and indigo, would suddenly appear from nowhere.

When Eleonora arrived at the hotel, she unpacked her bag and went out to explore, walking down dusty dirt roads dotted with small stones. Every person she came across gave her a wide smile, as if welcoming her. She was overcome by a feeling of peace, felt welcomed, and was sure that she could be lulled by the slow rhythm of that strip of land.

Eleonora walked on until she reached Coconut Beach. It was almost sunset. On that piece of land unique to the planet, from which one could admire the rising moon and the setting sun at the same time, she decided to go for a swim. She desperately wanted to dive into nature, to become part of that pale beach and the ocean. She closed her eyes and swam, searching for purification. *Could this place, so strongly dedicated to spirituality provide some balm for my heart?* she wondered.

A small group of young Indian women was bathing in the same stretch of water. They peeked at her from under their eyelashes, giggling. They were not used to seeing a half-naked woman in the sea. Each was dressed in a sari, which turned a shade darker in the water.

Eleonora was equally fascinated by these women who seemed so serene and composed, especially compared to the women of New York. Their movements were languorous; time didn't hurry their rhythm. This was what she needed— patience and calm—and she had found both in that place. The sun had set, orange and red streaks playing across the sky amid the clouds, providing an enchanted light.

Eleonora came out of the water, took her bag, and stopped close to an elderly woman sitting on the beach. She was selling flowers, which were carefully laid out on large banana leaves. Eleonora bought a garland of white flowers, placed it on her head, said a few words, and turned to go. The elderly lady brought her hands together at heart height and said "Namaste." Eleonora thanked her and went off towards Satsangam.

Walking back, she found herself thinking about the woman's face. It reminded her of a long time ago, as if she had always known her, her eyes conveying volumes more than Eleonora's hesitant English. She copied the greeting the woman had made, with her hands together and head bent forward. *Namaste*, she repeated to herself.

There wasn't a real reception area at the Satsangam Lodge; in the large entrance hall was a desk where information regarding the arrivals and departures of the guests could be obtained. Marise was standing there when Eleonora asked, "Marise, what does 'Namaste' mean?"

"I bow to the godhead that is in you!" she answered.

Eleonora headed off towards her hut, breathing in the godhead in her deeply, smiling. She saw herself reflected in a mirror and examined herself with new eyes; for a moment she wondered if she had godhead within her somewhere. She felt more like a clown with the garland of flowers still in her hair, but the concept of godhead was working inside her somewhere, on a subtle plane.

She went to bed early that night, in part because of jet lag, but also because the center followed the natural rhythms of the day. Breakfast was served at six o'clock, followed by meditation, various holistic activities, and Kathakali courses for those interested. There was no electric light; the intention was to live in a dimension out of time, following the natural cycle of the sun. The Ayurvedic cuisine was aimed at balancing the five elements of space, air, fire, water, and earth that constitute the human body. Eleonora's simple hut was made of plaited giant palm leaves and contained a straw chair and a bed.

She lay down and watched the swaths of moonlight filter onto her body through the gaps in the plaited leaves. The cicadas and fireflies accompanied her thoughts with their songs. She was reminded of Claire's words to her before her departure. "Ele, come on. It's overrated and banal to go to India to find yourself. Just find the right man and you'll forget the past. With good sex, you'll find yourself." Only now could she find the right words to answer. For a soul weakened by sickness, India is like an ablution in spirituality. It may be banal, but at times you need to go physically to a specific place to follow an internal process and encourage a total immersion. Spiritual lethargy is not easy to shake in New York.

She knew she was in the right place. Her thoughts began to take shape in that hut; she could perceive a higher feeling, a feeling that was part of the universe. She fell asleep full of hope.

THE LIGHT OF DAWN

Awakened by the dawn light, Eleonora put aside her usual clothing and chose a sari. Barefoot, she joined the other guests in a sun salute, following which they were served an Ayurvedic breakfast. Then she went to town. She spent the morning with a wholesaler in his store of precious fabrics.

She decided that the colors of India would inspire the summer collection. She examined some raw silk; in her mind, she was picturing a piece that would best show off the fabric. She was enchanted by the shantung silks in saffron, ivory, and gold, mentally sketching evening dresses, and stared at the lilacs and pinks with visions of bridal dresses in her head. Never before had she found inspiration for an entire collection in such a short time. She quickly sketched the pieces on some paper she found so she wouldn't forget them, satisfied with the fabrics she had chosen. They would be delivered to the showroom in a couple of days.

She decided to return to Coconut Beach, feeling that she had earned a restorative swim. She walked into the water in her sari, wanting to understand what the Indian women felt.

With her body weighed down, she found it hard to swim, and so let herself travel on the waves, drifting. Her sari floated out in the water, unrolling. She could feel the weight of the fabric gradually sloughing off her until she was naked. Her hair was moving in the rocking of the waves; her ears were underwater, and she could hear her amplified breathing. She breathed in and out, entering into symbiosis with the rhythm of the sea and the earth, in a new consciousness. Her thoughts stilled. When she came to, she swam with difficulty to shore, dragging her clothing behind her.

The elderly flower lady was sitting on the beach in the lotus position, her flowers already laid out carefully on the palm trays. The vivid colors enchanted Eleonora; she had never seen such intensely colorful and strongly scented blooms before.

"Namaste" she said, her hands together. "Namaste" answered the flower lady, her eyes staring at the sun beginning to set. Before Eleonora could wonder whether she should sit or not, she found herself sitting cross-legged next to the woman. She felt attracted by the vibrations that the woman emanated. They spent a long time in silence, staring at the sun on the sea, and then the woman said, "Tell me."

Eleonora's heart was beating loudly; her thoughts were jumbled and confused. Pictures of her life—faded moments that she had forgotten—suddenly flashed into her mind. She felt as if she were going down a tunnel full of water in which she was floating backwards, quickly. She began to remember her childhood.

Eleonora began to tell the woman about her life. She started with short sentences, which rapidly became a rush of consciousness—Villino Maddalena on the beach, the Turkish Steps, the warning in the tornado, her mother's attempted suicide, Venice and the moment of truth about Alex's ASD, Bob, Phil, and her father's attempt to claim back his son. She tried to put every piece of the puzzle of her life into the right place to find the sense of it all.

"There is a hidden side to everything," said the woman. "What happens to us in life is necessary because we need to understand something. You have dedicated your life to your family, but now your task ends here. Think about the evolution of your own soul; you can't decide for others. It is just a dance of souls—the karma between your father and your brother, between your mother and your father, is very heavy, and comes from long ago. Don't think about the pain. You may only let go of the suffering through love for your father. He is the other side of your brother. Love him without anger, as you love your brother. Alex will decide where to live."

"How will I know where that is?"

"Ask him without treating him as ill; otherwise, you are

behaving like your father."

"I get the idea."

"If you are ready to face life and solitude, cut off your past without making judgments, without regrets, and without resentment or revenge. Be still in the silence and solitude to see how much anger there is inside you and how to transform it. Solitude will clarify things for you." The woman's voice had a peaceful, constant rhythm. "Now you must rebuild your existence, but you must be careful not to fall into old habits. Physical manifestations are important because they offer support." She was shining with light.

Eleonora kept every word she said in her heart, like a precious gem in a secret box, although she hadn't understood everything. She sat in silence, watching the colors of the sunset. She had never felt so good in her life, and she was sure that she would keep forever the memory of the wonderful light show she was watching. She had never had a strong faith in anything in particular, except an irresistible attraction for nature. But she had allowed the woman to enter her world and allowed herself to be transported by her energy.

After a long silence, the woman began to speak again. "One needs humility to reach God. Develop the virtues that are in you. The time for feeling guilty about your family is over; each of them must follow their own path, and you, yours. You can no longer manage or interfere in their lives.

Leave behind your old consciousness. Past experiences are necessary to you to learn from and to change old thoughts. Everything is useful for your evolution."

"Do you think I can have healthy children, or are my genes damaged?" asked Eleonora.

"There is no such thing as genetics," replied the woman. "Genes are useful to enable living through a particular experience. One inherits an illness only because one must learn from it. It is karma that decides, not that genetics has linked you to something. Genetics make karma possible, just as sickness is the pathway to reach death."

"Why does my father not want Alex to be treated?"

There was another long silence. Fishermen were pulling their boats onto shore, moving with expertise, in unison, as if they had already repeated those gestures many, many times before. The elderly lady began to speak again in her slow, measured pace. "It is the dance of souls that cannot be seen by the human eye. What happens between them is probably what must happen. All parents have specific responsibilities for the evolution of their children. The heavy karma between your father and Alex is blocking evolution. If you are ready to face life and solitude, cut off your past without making judgments, without regrets, and without resentment or revenge," the woman repeated. "Cut free and breathe; cut free and realize how much each of us has the right to be where we are."

Images of her past life came tumbling seamlessly forward before her eyes, like a collage of old photos. And, like a puzzle in which the last piece has finally placed, Eleonora began to understand more. Her conscience finally started to find peace. She no longer judged her father's behavior; she simply had to accept it. Beside the sea, her anger was dissolving. She had never entered into contact with the spiritual; she had always nourished her mind and her body, but never her soul. She felt that this unknown side could provide energy for her heart.

The woman handed her some flowers. Eleonora got to her feet and walked into the water, up to her knees. She offered the flowers to the sea, thanking the universe and the gods for understanding and for a peace she had never before felt. She dropped the petals into the waves. With her eyes closed, she cut her emotional umbilical cord forever and breathed the vibrations of a new start amid the waters of the ocean.

A WOMAN'S TEARS ARE PRECIOUS

Alessandro like Luigi, Luigi like Alessandro. There was no need to fight any longer; no need to fight battles for others. Eleonora had learned to trust and be brave. The elderly woman's words, "the power of the soul is infinite," echoed through her head. She wanted to choose to live in love. She had chosen love in every circumstance; love for everyone, kindness that attracted kindness, gentleness that kept the darkness at bay.

Several days later, Eleonora returned to New York. She felt an urgent need to spend time with Alex. She went to the center and found him changed; he seemed sadder and calmer, but happy to see his sister. They walked in the garden and then sat on a bench. There were children of all ages with serious physical and mental disorders roaming the garden with no precise goal. Every now and again someone would come up to the bench and socialize with Eleonora, each in his or her own way. Some of them already knew her as the sister of their friend Alessandro.

The first to come up was Massimo, who was fifteen years old. He repeated his stereotypes continually, like a stuck record, always replicating the same sentence accompanied by the same gesture. It wasn't always easy to keep one's patience with him. Alex appeared to understand that, saying, "Oh, oh, Mimi, life is hard!"

Eleonora answered, "You're right, but it is lovely, too!"

Then it was John's turn. He ran to their bench and hugged Eleonora, saying, "I love you, mummy."

"Go away, child, go," said Alex. "Leave Mimi you."

David stared into the distance, his head slightly cocked to one side. His drool made a transparent thread that reached his trousers. He was in a wheelchair pushed by his caregiver. Then Rose approached, somersaulting forward and across. Always overexcited and brimming with energy, she had a good grasp of language and would proposition every boy. "Will you make zum zum with me?" Her caregiver did not lose sight of her for a moment.

Alex's favorite was his friend Matthieu, a handsome boy in his twenties with indigo eyes and blonde curls. He expressed himself only in poetry and verses, which he would make up on the spot. That day he dedicated a thought to Eleonora.

Every time that you feel like crying,
Every time you cry, I will want to be there with you,
Facing you, with my face very close to yours.
So many tears that drop from your eyes,
My sweetest love.
They are precious to be wasted, to fall to the ground.
I want to be there to gather them all and bring them to my face,
So I can keep them like an ambrosia inside of me.
A woman's tears are precious.

Alex burst out laughing and said, "Shut up, you idiot, don't be a clown."

"I have to go to my drawing now. I take my leave, princess" said Matthieu, heading off.

"Thank you Matthieu. See you soon! Write down everything that comes into your head. You are very clever," Eleonora called after him.

She took Alex's hand and, for the first time, talked to him seriously. "Papa wants you to go back to his house. What do you want to do?"

Alex stared into her eyes and answered, "I go home. Papa cry, I cry."

Eleonora reminded herself of the woman's words; "Cut free and breathe, cut free and realize how each of us has the right to be where they are." Alessandro had made his choice with great sincerity. He wanted to go home to Sicily to his father, and Eleonora had chosen to respect her brother's choice.

"Okay, my dear heart. We'll leave in a couple of days. Get your bags ready."

"Yes, tanks Mimi. I want home," answered Alex joyfully.

"I'LL NEVER FORGET YOU"

Threatened by Luigi with the prospect of being homeless without financial support, Letizia accepted the proposal that Alex return to his father's home, but she didn't fully understand that this was also what her son wanted. "It's okay by me for you to take him," said Letizia, "but if my husband doesn't even know how to find the cutlery, how on earth is he going to look after your brother? The two of them are going to kill each other. I tell you, we'll find them both dead! My husband is the sick one. And I can already see the headlines—'Man kills autistic son and then himself.' He will be forever on my conscience."

"Well, you managed to deal with him for years! And you're still calling him 'my husband.' 'Ex,' Mamma, 'ex-husband.' You're separated."

"Husband or ex-husband, he's still the same madman! And be careful—your father always said that he would leave everything to Luigino's family on his death so that they would take care of Alex. And that good-for-nothing Phil! He was supposed to get me a good settlement, but no, he got taken for a ride by Luigi. What a spineless man, a waste of time! At least your father doesn't let his mind be changed by the first person who comes by."

"And that, Mamma, is the problem. My father has never listened to anyone. I agree that Phil has no courage, but the poor thing wasn't strong enough. What can you do?"

"Me? Nothing. But if a man even dares to come close, I will kill him with a glance. All men are to stay far away from me."

Several days later, they went to the center to pick up Alex. He was waiting anxiously for them at the entrance. "Good Mamma, good Mimi" he shouted happily, jumping up and down on the spot in his inimitable way. Eleonora got out of the car, ran over to her brother and began jumping up and down with him. With every jump, they laughed and shouted out together: "'Uck, dick, bum, prick, bloody hell, shit, balls, 'uck you."[18] And they counted the insults on their fingers as they said them until they got to ten—like the commandments.

"Be quiet, you two! They'll think we're mad!" Letizia shushed them.

"We are all mad, yes we are!" added Eleonora.

---

[18] "Fuck, dick, bum, prick, bloody hell, shit, balls, fuck you."

Alex repeated with her, "All mad, yesss. Me go papa. Yesss."

"Go and get your bag," said Letizia.

Alex ran toward the building. On the porch, the patients and caregivers of the center were waiting to say goodbye to Alessandro. They counted to three, then launched into "Vincerò," which they knew was Alex's favorite song. He was still jumping up and down, saying, "Thank you guys, my friends." Some of them hugged him rather emotionally, others made the gestures they usually did when joking together, some gave him a high-five, yet others hugged him, and a few mimed his drum playing. Each in their own way, they all said goodbye. Still thanking them, Alex walked over to the car with his mother and sister and got in. They drove off, followed by the kids, who ran behind them as the gate closed. Alex turned around to see them all climbing up the gate at different heights. "'Bye Alex, take care, think of us when you play the drums, don't forget us!" they called.

I will never forget you, thought Alex, a tear rolling down his face.

THE BORDER

Eleonora and Alessandro landed at the airport in Palermo on a hot, sunny day in mid-May, and then took a taxi to Agrigento. On the journey, they were pleasantly impressed by the Sicilian countryside, which they had almost forgotten. Eleonora tried to prepare a speech to make to her father when they met, but couldn't find the right words.

When they reached the long, tree-lined drive that lead up to the villa, time seemed to stretch out. Eleonora grabbed her diary, scribbling quickly: *Every time I have walked through the gates to my parent's house, my heart has stopped beating for a second, my mind has dimmed and emptied, no thoughts daring to show their faces. It is almost as if the gates are a point that mark the border between the macrocosm with all that it offers—vitality, lively rhythm, and the opportunity to make my dreams come true. And on the other side is the microcosm, this huge, majestic villa that devours, kills, and erodes, slowly and gradually. In the microcosm, life is pushed aside, joy forbidden, and sex, for God's sake, not even allowed by mistake or in error. It must have been the least-used word in the house. That microcosm is filled with fear, icy stares, heavy silences, fists that damage, psychic, physical, and verbal violence, and a sense of waiting for death.*

That microcosm, triumphant in its pain, untreatable in its suffering, which I have always hated and refused, has today melted away. It has finally liquefied, like a soap bubble, like the one that lasts the longest, the one you think will never burst. But then it does, and a smile spreads on the face of the child who was watching it. From today there will be new life in this microcosm—Alex and that drum kit, just waiting to be played.

Two summers ago, the last time I came through these gates, everything I witnessed made me beg my ex-boyfriend to take me as far away as possible from that nightmare, and I swore to myself that I would never return. A slatted white gate, a weeping willow standing before the beautiful sea, the African coastline on the horizon. Today it is all different. Only at the end of the journey do you understand the structure of life. You can look at it from the outside, objectively, as if it weren't yours, and understand all the reasons. You can put all the pieces together to finally close the circle. Then you can start again, looking at the people and events from a different perspective. Then you realize that nothing happens by chance and everything serves to grow, to evolve, to develop.

"Keep the change," said Eleonora as they got out of the taxi. The gate opened and they walked to the front door, pulling their suitcases. Eleonora paused to look at the swing, the sea, the palm trees, the engraved stone, the tennis court.

Everything was unchanged, just rendered more opaque and rough by another layer of sea salt—a sign of time passing, like Luigi's grey hair, which moved towards Alex's as he bent to hug him after so long. He was emotional, listening to Alex's account of the journey. "Plane, Uncle Gigi, lovely, New Yo' skyscrapers, very high, lots of lights. How do you do? Me speak American."

"Really? You're all grown up," said his father.

Luigi hugged Eleonora tightly. "Thank you, Mimi, I can't live without you two."

Eleonora felt a strong rush of affection for her father, and her resentment and anger towards the old man dissolved. She loved her father like she loved Alex, and only now did she recognize the strange behavior of each. Because Alex's characteristics were so clearly demonstrated, she had understood them immediately; Luigi's strangeness was hidden, so she had needed thirty years to recognize and finally accept it.

"Just promise me one thing, Papa. Never give care of Alex to Luigino's family or to anyone else. When you think you can't manage any longer, I will come and get him and he will stay with me. You don't know what other people could do; they don't know him. Don't create any more negative situations, please! If you leave everything to a stranger in exchange for their help with Alex, they could take your money and the house and leave my brother on the street. And how could I prevent that? I am not interested in an inheritance, but please make sure that Alex doesn't lose out. He doesn't know how to defend himself, and I don't think I do, either. If it is true that you live for us, show me that you do."

"I will take care of my family; you think about making one of your own," answered her father.

Eleonora took a deep breath and decided to let that provoking remark drop. She went into the kitchen where Maddalena was still exclaiming over Alex. She hugged her tightly, saying, "Granny, you're looking wonderful. Your red lipstick is always perfect."

"Us girls, we like to keep in shape," answered Maddalena.

"How are you, Granny?"

"An old lady," she replied. "I keep going. Every day of life is one more day conquered. I am so happy that you have brought your brother. When is your mother coming?"

"Granny, I don't think that Mamma will ever come back. She's fine, but still being treated for Parkinson's."

Luigi interrupted, "What do you mean, Parkinson's? Your mother is perfectly healthy; she has just found an excuse to get rid of her son. She could shame a Hollywood actress."

"Papa, please, don't agitate Alex," Eleonora cautioned, and then turned to her brother and said, "Come on, Alex, let's go and play tennis."

Maddalena added, "Tell your mother she needs to come back! When I die, how is my son going to cope in this big house all alone?"

"Okay, Granny, I'll tell her."

Eleonora had hated that villa ever since the tornado. Now, though, she no longer felt agitated. She knew that she had never fully belonged to that place. Since she was a child, she had always wondered why she had been born into that family, and now she understood why.

She enjoyed herself, playing with her brother as they had done as children. That was the last time she played tennis with Alessandro in that house. The next day she returned to New York, ready to work on the new collection.

ACKNOWLEDGMENTS

My heartfelt thanks go to those who have supported me and believed in this book:

Francesca Angrisano, President of the Academy of Pranic Healing, Rome, without whom nothing would've ever have happened.
www.accademiapranichealing.it

Dr. Nicola Antonucci and the Autism Research Institute, without whom I could not have learned many informations about and treatments for ASD.
www.emergenzaautismo.org
www.autism.com

Swami Kriyananda, Founder of the Ananda communities, for being my guide.
www.ananda.org

And my deepest thanks to:

Franco Nero, what an incredible honor to have someone of your caliber and status write such touching and meaningful comments.

Vincenzo Amato, I am humbled by the sensativity expressed by you towards my book. You are such a celebrated international artist.

Spencer Garrett, I was really moved by the kindness and compassion of your precious words.

Carlo Siliotto, for being the first reader in America who believed in my book.

Fabrizio Mancinelli, for composing your amazing music for the book-trailer:
https://www.youtube.com/watch?v=HW91mEGqQIY

ABOUT THE AUTHOR

Romina Caruana is an actress and author born in Agrigento, Sicily. She graduated, from the University of Palermo with a degree in Modern Languages, with the highest honors. She received her acting diploma from 'Teatès' drama academy in Palermo. She attended several workshops in 'Script Analysis', 'Script Writing' and 'Actor's Training' led by Michael Margotta at Actor's Center in Rome. She studied with Susan Batson at Black Nexxus Inc. in New York City, and Kathakali drama-dance at the 'Satsangam International Centre' for Art and Culture in Trivandrum-India. Miss Caruana is attending the 'New Collective' acting school with Greg Braun in Los Angeles, where she currently lives.

www.rominacaruana.com